Praise for the thrillers of Jack Higgins

BAD COMPANY

"Higgins writes with spare velocity, racing through a complex plot . . . [and] has no equal in the realm of ex-Nazis wreaking havoc. . . . Higgins maintains the suspense and even manages a series of nasty surprises along the way."
—*St. Louis Post-Dispatch*

"Fans will find enough gnarly action and sentiment here to make them anticipate [Higgins's] next." —*Publishers Weekly*

MIDNIGHT RUNNER

"The fun comes from the wisecracking band of dangerous but bighearted secret soldiers Higgins wheels out to save the world—and his galloping Hollywood-ready pace."
—*People*

"Swift and coursing with dark passion . . . as credible and steel-hearted as Higgins's best." —*Publishers Weekly*

EDGE OF DANGER

"This is Higgins near the top of his game . . . another winner." —*Publishers Weekly*

"His 32nd triumphant exercise in keeping readers hugely entertained." —*Los Angeles Times*

"The action is nonstop." —*Minneapolis Star Tribune*

continued . . .

DAY OF RECKONING

"The action is sleek and intensely absorbing, but the supreme pleasure is in those Higgins celebrates—tarnished warriors who value honor over life and who get the job done no matter what the cost." —*Publishers Weekly*

THE WHITE HOUSE CONNECTION

"The White House Connection has one heckuva heroine . . . [who] begins a one-woman assassination spree that will keep you turning the pages." —Larry King, *USA Today*

"Masterful . . . a satisfying, suspense-filled book." —*Roanoke Times & World News*

"[A] page-turning thriller." —*The Indianapolis Star*

THE PRESIDENT'S DAUGHTER

"A tight story with plenty of action." —*Chattanooga Free Press*

NIGHT JUDGEMENT AT SINOS

"This is one you won't put down." —*The New York Times*

DRINK WITH THE DEVIL

"A most intoxicating thriller." —The Associated Press

"It is Dillon's likability and the author's adroitness in giving his character the room he needs that make Higgins's novels so readable." —*The Washington Times*

YEAR OF THE TIGER

"Higgins spins as mean a tale as Ludlum, Forsythe, or any of them." — *Philadelphia Daily News*

ANGEL OF DEATH

"Pulsing excitement . . . Higgins makes the pages fly." — *New York Daily News*

"The action never stops." — *The San Francisco Examiner*

EYE OF THE STORM
Also published as *Midnight Man*

"Heart-stopping . . . spectacular and surprising." — *Abilene Reporter-News*

"Razor-edged . . . will give you an adrenaline high. It's a winner." — *Tulsa World*

ON DANGEROUS GROUND

"A whirlwind of action, with a hero who can out-Bond old James. It's told in the author's best style, with never a pause for breath." — *The New York Times Book Review*

SHEBA

"When it comes to thriller writers, one name stands well above the crowd—Jack Higgins." — The Associated Press

THUNDER POINT

"Dramatic . . . authentic . . . one of the author's best." — *The New York Times*

"A rollicking adventure that twists and turns." — *The San Diego Union-Tribune*

DARK JUSTICE

JACK HIGGINS

BERKLEY BOOKS, NEW YORK

THE BERKLEY PUBLISHING GROUP
Published by the Penguin Group
Penguin Group (USA) Inc.
375 Hudson Street, New York, New York 10014, USA

Penguin Group (Canada), 10 Alcorn Avenue, Toronto, Ontario M4V 3B2, Canada
(a division of Pearson Penguin Canada Inc.)
Penguin Books Ltd., 80 Strand, London WC2R 0RL, England
Penguin Group Ireland, 25 St. Stephen's Green, Dublin 2, Ireland (a division of Penguin Books Ltd.)
Penguin Group (Australia), 250 Camberwell Road, Camberwell, Victoria 3124, Australia
(a division of Pearson Australia Group Pty. Ltd.)
Penguin Books India Pvt. Ltd., 11 Community Centre, Panchsheel Park, New Delhi—110 017, India
Penguin Group (NZ), Cnr. Airborne and Rosedale Roads, Albany, Auckland 1310, New Zealand
(a division of Pearson New Zealand Ltd.)
Penguin Books (South Africa) (Pty.) Ltd., 24 Sturdee Avenue, Rosebank, Johannesburg 2196,
South Africa

Penguin Books Ltd., Registered Offices: 80 Strand, London WC2R 0RL, England

This is a work of fiction. Names, characters, places, and incidents either are the product of the author's imagination or are used fictitiously, and any resemblance to actual persons, living or dead, business establishments, events, or locales is entirely coincidental.

DARK JUSTICE

A Berkley Book / published by arrangement with HarperCollins Publishers, Ltd.

PRINTING HISTORY
G. P. Putnam's Sons hardcover edition / August 2004
Berkley international edition / April 2005

Copyright © 2004 by Harry Patterson.
Cover design and digital illustration copyright © 2004 by Rob Wood/Wood Ronsaville and Harlin, Inc.

ISBN: 0-425-20362-X

BERKLEY®
Berkley Books are published by The Berkley Publishing Group,
a division of Penguin Group (USA) Inc.,
375 Hudson Street, New York, New York 10014.
BERKLEY is a registered trademark of Penguin Group (USA) Inc.
The "B" design is a trademark belonging to Penguin Group (USA) Inc.

PRINTED IN THE UNITED STATES OF AMERICA

10 9 8 7 6 5 4 3 2 1

One sword is worth
ten thousand words.

— THE KORAN

NEW YORK

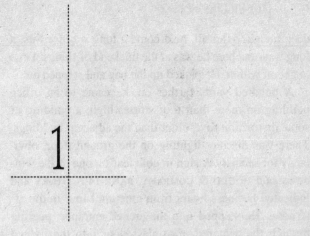

1

Manhattan on a dark November evening around eight o'clock was bleak and uninviting, an east wind driving heavy rain before it, as Henry Morgan turned the corner of a side street into Park Avenue.

He was a small man wearing a dark blue uniform and cap with the legend ICON SECURITY emblazoned on each shoulder; in one hand was a black leather bag, and the other held an umbrella over his head.

Park Avenue was hardly deserted at that hour, cars swishing by, although there were few pedestrians because of the rain. He turned into a convenient doorway for a moment and looked each way. It was a mixture of offices and residences, mostly impressive town houses, lights at the windows. He'd always loved cities by night and felt a sudden nostalgia, emotional of course, and he took a deep breath. After all, he'd come a long way for this, a long way, and here he was at the final end of things. Time to get on with it. He picked up the bag and stepped out.

A hundred yards farther on, he came to an office building no more than four stories high, a building of some distinction to it, older than the adjacent buildings. There was discreet lighting on the ground floor, obviously for security. A sign in gold leaf on one of the windows said GOULD & COMPANY, BANK DEPOSITORY and indicated business hours from nine until four in the afternoon. He stepped into the arched entrance, peering through the armored plate-glass door into the lighted foyer, and pressed the buzzer for Chesney, only Chesney didn't come. Instead, a large black man wearing the same dark blue uniform appeared and opened the door.

"Hey, you're late. Morgan, isn't it? The English guy? Chesney told me about you."

Morgan stepped inside. The door closed noiselessly behind him. A bad start, but he'd have to make the best of it.

"I'm sorry. I always get Chesney coffee and sandwiches from a place round the corner." He followed the other man through to the reception area. "Where is he?"

"The way I heard it, his gallbladder's playing up again, so they rushed me over from South Street."

"What do I call you?"

"Smith will do." He sat behind the desk, took out a pack of Marlboros and lit one. "A busy night out there, but at least there are a couple of good movies on TV. So you're from London, they tell me?"

"That's right."

"So what are you doing over here?"

"Oh, pastures new, you know how it is."

"Lucky you got a green card."

"Well, I'd been doing this kind of thing over there. It helped."

Smith nodded. "Anyway, let's see what you've got in that bag." Morgan's stomach turned hollow and he hesitated. Smith reached for the bag. "I'm starving, and what with them rushing me over here at the last minute, I had no chance to get anything."

Morgan hurriedly pulled the bag up, put it on the desk, opened it, produced coffee and sandwiches and passed them over.

"What about you?" Smith asked.

"I'll have mine later. I'll do the rounds first."

"Suit yourself." Smith started to unwrap a sandwich.

"I'll get started, then. I'll just drop my bag in the rest room."

He moved to the other end of the foyer and did just that, then called to Smith, "See you later."

"Take your time." Smith switched on the television, and Morgan entered the elevator and pressed the buttons that took him down to the vault.

He checked it thoroughly, giving what he'd put in the coffee time to work, although the effect was almost instantaneous and good for five hours, or so they'd told him. He trawled the vault, hundreds of steel boxes behind bars, went back to the elevator and ascended to the fourth floor.

It was all office accommodation, everything in good order, and it was the same when he went down to the third and then the second floor. Boring, really, to have to spend your working life doing this. But it would soon be over. He returned to the elevator and went down.

Smith was slumped across the desk, out completely, the partly drunk coffee cup beside him. The sandwich had a couple of bites out of it, but that was all. Morgan shook him to make sure, then turned to the general security box and switched it off for the entire building. He went along to the rest room, retrieved his bag, got into the elevator and went to the second floor.

When he went out, he dimmed the lights, walked across to the window looking out over Park Avenue to the splendid town house on the other side, its many windows ablaze with lights. Parking had been banned for the whole block, and not just because it was owned by Senator Harvey Black.

Having switched off the entire alarm system, Morgan was able to open the control panel by the window without any unseemly fuss. He started to whistle softly, put the bag on the table, opened it and produced an AK-47, unfolded the stock, cocked it and laid it across the windowsill, checking his watch.

It was twenty to nine and the fund-raiser at the Pierre would just be finishing. Senator Black would be bringing his honored guest back to the house for dinner at nine o'clock.

Morgan took a pack of cigarettes from his pocket, lit one and sat there at the open window, cradling the AK-47 with every intention of shooting the President of the United States dead the moment he stepped out on the pavement.

Suddenly, he heard the sound of the elevator in operation below. For a moment, he froze in a kind of panic, then jumped to his feet and turned to face the elevator. It stopped and Smith stepped out, followed by a tall, handsome man of fifty or so, black hair graying.

"Why, Henry," Smith said. "What's all this? I didn't see anything about it in the job description."

Morgan backed away, thinking hard.

There was a pause and the other man said, "Mr. Morgan, my name is Blake Johnson. I work for the President of the United States. This gentleman is Clancy Smith of the Secret Service. I regret to tell you that the President isn't coming tonight. Seems he canceled the dinner at the last moment and flew back to Washington. So sorry."

He stepped forward and, in a single motion, Morgan raised the AK and fired at point-blank range—but only the rattle of the bolt sounded.

Smith said, "Forgot to mention. I emptied it when you went down to the vault. And by the way—I never accept coffee from strangers."

Morgan dropped the AK to the floor with a look of despair on his face. Johnson almost felt sorry for him.

"Hell, man, we got Saddam Hussein. Did you really think *you* could pull this off? Anything to say?"

"Yes," Morgan said. "Beware the Wrath of Allah."

He seemed to bite hard, his jaw tightening, then he staggered back, tripped and fell to the floor, moaning terribly, his face contorted. There was a strange, pungent smell as Smith dropped to one knee and peered closely at him. He glanced up, "I don't know what in the hell that smell is, but this guy is dead."

By special arrangement, Blake had the body removed by army paramedics and conveyed to an exclusive private hospital used mainly for rehab patients. It did, however, offer state-of-the-art morgue facilities and he'd called in one of New York's finest chief medical examiners, Dr. George Romano, to do the necessary.

He and Clancy had stopped off at their hotel so that Clancy could change from the security uniform, and arrived at their destination a good hour after the corpse and found Romano in the Superintendent's office already garbed for action. He and Blake were old friends. Romano had done a lot of work for the Basement, the White House security organization that Johnson ran. Romano was drinking coffee and smoking.

"I thought that was against the law these days, especially for doctors."

"Around here I make my own rules, Blake. Who's your friend?"

"Clancy Smith, Secret Service. He's taken a bullet for the President in the past. Fortunately, nothing like that was needed tonight."

"I've started on our friend, Mr. Morgan. Just taking a break."

"John Doe, if you don't mind," Blake said.

"And what if I do?"

Blake turned to Clancy, who opened the briefcase he carried, took out a document and passed it across to the doctor.

"You'll notice that's addressed to one George Romano and signed by President Jake Cazalet. It's what's called a 'presidential warrant.' It says you belong to the President, it transcends all our laws, and you can't even say no. You also never discuss what happened tonight, because it never happened."

For once, Romano wasn't smiling. "That bad?" He shook his head. "I should have known when I realized you'd given me a Heinrich Himmler."

"What in the hell is that supposed to mean?" Clancy demanded.

"I'll go back in and show you if you can stand to watch."

"I was in Vietnam and Clancy was in the Gulf. I think we can stand it," Blake said.

"Excuse me, I was in 'Nam, too," said Romano, "and with all due respect, the Gulf War was pussy."

"Yeah, well, Clancy here has got two Navy Crosses to prove otherwise," Blake said. "But let's get on with it."

In the postmortem room, two technicians waited while Romano scrubbed up again. He was helped into surgical gloves and moved to the naked body of Henry Morgan, who lay on the slanting steel table, his head raised high on a wooden block, the mouth gaping. Close at hand were a video recorder and an instrument cart.

Romano said, "Wednesday, November third, resuming postmortem, Henry Morgan, address unknown." He turned to Blake and Clancy. "Come closer. Because of the unusual circumstances, I decided to investigate the mouth first, and if you look closely you'll find a molar missing at the left side."

He pulled the mouth open with a finger and disclosed the bloodied gap.

"And here it is, gents." He picked up a small stainless-steel pan and rattled the crushed remains of a tooth in it that was part gold. "Heinrich Himmler, for the benefit of those too young to remember, was Reichsführer of the SS during the immortal days of the Third Reich. However, he was smart enough to know that all good things come to an end and didn't fancy the hangman's noose. So he had a false tooth fitted that contained a cyanide capsule. A number of Nazis did. Faced with capture, you crunch down as hard as you can. Death is virtually instantaneous."

"So our friend here had no intention of being taken alive?"

"I'd say so. Now, in spite of the fact that I suspect it will prove useless, I intend to complete my usual thorough examination. What, by the way, do you know about the guy?"

"The only thing I can tell you is that he's thirty years old. When can I have the body?"

"I'd say an hour should do it."

"Good. I'll arrange transportation while we're waiting in the office, and George . . ." He pulled him away and murmured softly, "I don't mind the technicians having heard the Himmler bit, but nothing more. No comment. And bring the videotape when you're finished."

"Yes, O great one."

Romano turned back to the task at hand, and Blake and Clancy went out.

They sat in the Superintendent's office, and Blake made a call on his Codex mobile. It was answered almost instantly.

"Highgrove."

"It's Blake Johnson, I phoned earlier about a disposal."

"Of course, sir. We're ready and waiting."

"You know where we are. The package will be ready in one hour."

"We'll be there."

"And I'll expect the disposal to be immediate."

"Naturally."

Blake switched off. "Let's have some coffee."

There was a pot standing ready in the machine. Clancy went and poured two cups. "Not a thing on him. Swept clean. No ID, no passport, and yet he had to have one to get into the country."

"Probably stashed it before he came here tonight. Everything else was likely forged. Came into the country posing as a tourist. A forged green card was supplied, a room booked for him in some modest hotel."

"And the AK?"

"Could have been left for him in a locker anywhere. The job at the security agency could have been arranged for him in advance. I'll bet he didn't even meet anyone from his organization here in New York."

"But some outfit sent him from London."

"Of course, otherwise why would he be here? They've probably got friends in New York who kept an anonymous eye on him, but preferred not to get involved."

"I wouldn't blame them. It was a suicide mission," Clancy said. "Even if we hadn't gotten him now, he'd have been run down like a dog if the worst had happened."

"Very probably. Now I must speak to the President."

He found Cazalet at his desk in the Oval Office.

"Mr. President, we got him. The whole thing was for real. He's dead, unfortunately."

"That is unfortunate. Gunshot wound?"

"Cyanide."

"Dear me. Where are you now?"

"The mortuary, waiting for the disposal team."

"Fine. Take care of it, Blake. This never happened. I don't want it on the front page of the *New York Times*. I'll order a plane to pick up you and Clancy. I want you back here as soon as possible so we can sort things out."

"Yes, Mr. President."

"And since it was our British cousins who alerted us to the existence of Morgan, you'd better telephone General Ferguson and let him know."

In London, it was four o'clock in the morning when the security phone rang at General Charles Ferguson's flat in Cavendish Place. He switched on the bedside light and answered.

"At such an appalling hour, I can only assume this is of supreme importance."

"It always is when it concerns the Empire, Charles."

It was the code word used to indicate the President in danger.

Ferguson was fully alert now and sat up. "Blake, my good friend. What happened?"

"Your information on Henry Morgan was dead-on. He tried to hit the President tonight, but Clancy and I stopped him. Unfortunately, he had a cyanide tooth, so he's no longer with us."

"Is the President all right?"

"Absolutely. As for Morgan, what's left of him will soon be six pounds of gray ash. I'll probably flush it down the toilet."

"You're a hard man, Blake, harder than I believed possible."

"It's the nature of the job, Charles, and the bastard did intend to assassinate the President. Anyway, thanks to you and the rest of the Prime Minister's Private Army, it's all come out fine. Thank them all for me: Hannah Bernstein, Sean Dillon, and Major Roper."

"Especially Roper on this one. The man's a genius on the computer."

"Got to run, Charles. I'll be in touch."

Blake put the phone down, and Romano entered carrying a videotape and several documents.

"Good man," Blake said.

"Not really." Romano lit a cigarette. "I'm smart enough to know my place, that's all."

Clancy had gone out to check the corridor and found two men in black coats pushing a gurney with a body bag on it.

One of them, a quietly cadaverous man, said, "Mr. Johnson?"

Blake leaned out of the office door. "He's all ready and waiting for you. Load him on and we'll see you at Highgrove. Tell Mr. Coffin to wait until we arrive."

"As you say, sir."

They moved away. Clancy said, "Coffin? Is that for real?"

"If it's the man I know, it certainly is." Romano smiled bleakly. "Fergus Coffin. I believe it's called life imitating art." At that moment, the gurney returned with what was obviously Henry Morgan in the body bag. "On your way now, gentlemen. I think I've had enough for one night."

In the mortuary at Highgrove, Blake and Clancy waited by the ovens. Fergus Coffin and an attendant pushed the gurney forward, the body still enclosed in the black body bag.

Blake said, "Open it."

Coffin nodded and his associate unzipped it, exposing the head. Henry Morgan it was.

"He looks at peace," Blake said.

"He would be, Mr. Johnson," Coffin told him. "Death is a serious business. I've devoted my life to it."

"No questions?"

"None. I've seen the presidential warrant, but it's more than that. You're a good man, Mr. Johnson. Every instinct tells me that. You've known great sorrow."

Blake, remembering a murdered wife, stiffened for a moment and then said, "How long?"

"With the new technology, thirty minutes."

"Then get on with it. Put him in, but I need to see." He held out the documents and video. "And these."

The other man opened one of the oven doors, Coffin pushed the gurney forward, Henry Morgan slid inside. Coffin pulled the gurney away, the glass door closed, a button was pressed. The oven flared at once, the gas jets peaking, and the body bag flared instantly, also the video and documents.

Blake turned to Clancy. "We'll wait," and led the way outside.

In the office, they smoked cigarettes. Clancy said, "You want coffee?"

"Not in a million years. A good stiff drink is what I need, but we'll have to wait until we're on the plane."

Rain hammered against the window. Clancy said, "Does it ever bother you, this kind of thing?"

"Clancy, I went to war for my country in Vietnam when I was very young and full of ideals. I never really regretted it. Someone had to do it. Now, all these years later, we're at war with the world—a world where global terrorism is the name of the game." He stubbed out his cigarette in an ashtray. "And Clancy, I'll do anything it takes. I took an oath to my President and I take that to be an oath to my country." He smiled slightly. "Does that give you a problem?"

And Clancy Smith, once the youngest sergeant major in the Marine Corps, smiled. "Not in the slightest."

At that moment, the door opened and Coffin entered, holding a plastic urn. "Henry Morgan, six pounds of gray ash."

"Excellent," Blake said, and Clancy took the urn.

"Many thanks," Blake told Coffin. "Believe me, you've never done anything more important."

"I accept your word for that, Mr. Johnson," and Coffin went out.

"Let's go," Blake said, and added, "Bring the urn with you."

He led the way out to the parking lot, where the rain poured down relentlessly. They walked to their limousine, which was parked by what, in season, would obviously be a flower bed.

Blake said, "I was going to put those ashes down the toilet, but let's be more civilized and do something for next year's flowers."

"Good idea."

Clancy unscrewed the top of the urn and poured the ashes over the flower bed.

"I believe it's called strewing."

"I don't care what it's called. Washington next, so let's catch that plane."

WASHINGTON

2

But a cold front moving in from the Atlantic had done unmentionable things to the weather, and in spite of the rain, or because of it, low clouds produced heavy fog and closed things down at Kennedy.

Blake and Clancy made the best of things in one of the VIP lounges, dozing fitfully, but were still there at six the following morning when they got word that their Gulfstream had managed to get in.

As they walked out through the terminal, bags in hand, Clancy said, "There's no romance in this work anymore. I must have seen every James Bond movie on TV at one time or another, and he never got held up by bad weather at any airport, not once. Here we've got a Gulfstream, one of the classiest aircraft in the world, and it still couldn't get to us."

"Nature rules," Blake said. "Face up to it and shut up. We'll be on our way in fifteen minutes."

They rose up very quickly to thirty thousand feet. The crew was air force and their stewardess a young sergeant who introduced herself as Mary.

"Now, what can I get you gentlemen?"

"Well, I know it's only six-thirty in the morning," Blake told her, "but for very special reasons I think a bottle of champagne is in order. Could you manage that?"

"I think that could be arranged." She gave them a dazzling smile and moved down to the galley.

"We didn't do too badly, did we?" Clancy said. "Considering that the President could have been facedown on the pavement."

"That he isn't is due to Major Roper warning us that there was something fishy about Morgan in the first place. But I anticipated taking him alive, Clancy, squeezing the juice out of him."

"It's not your fault, Blake. We did everything right. The tooth thing was just unfortunate."

Sergeant Mary appeared with two glasses of champagne, which they took gratefully.

Blake toasted Clancy. "Let's hope the President agrees with you."

In Washington, the rain was even heavier when they arrived, but a limousine was waiting and they were taken through at once and on their way, moving along Constitution Avenue toward the White House. In spite of the weather, there was a sizable crowd of demonstrators, a kind of moonscape of umbrellas against the rain, shepherded by police.

"Which war are they protesting against?" Clancy asked.

"Who knows? There's some sort of war going on in nearly every country in the world these days. Don't ask me, Clancy. All I know is some people seem to make a profession out of protest."

The chauffeur lowered the glass screen that separated him from them. "Too difficult from the front, Mr. Johnson. May I try the East Entrance?"

"That's fine by me."

They turned up East Executive Avenue and stopped at the gate. Blake leaned out and the guard, recognizing him at once, waved them through. The East Entrance was much used by White House staff, especially when wishing to avoid the media. The limousine pulled up, Blake and Clancy got out and went up the steps. A young marine lieutenant was on duty, and a Secret Service agent named Huntley greeted them warmly.

"Mr. Johnson, Clancy. You're looking stretched, if I may say so."

"Don't ask," Blake said. "We spent most of the night stranded by fog at Kennedy, and the President's expecting us."

"You know where he is, sir, but I'll lead the way. It'll give my legs some exercise."

The President's secretary, a pleasant woman in her mid-forties, admitted them to the Oval Office, where they found Jake Cazalet in shirtsleeves at the desk, working his way through a raft of documents, reading glasses perched on the end of his nose. He glanced up, smiled.

"The return of the heroes. Have you eaten?"

"Early breakfast at Kennedy. Congealed scrambled eggs and fries at five-thirty, and that was the VIP lounge," Blake said.

Cazalet laughed and turned to the secretary. "We can manage our own coffee, Millie, but speak to the chef and find them something exotic like bacon sandwiches."

"Of course, Mr. President."

She withdrew, and the President said, "Okay, gentlemen. Let's hear the worst."

"The worst didn't happen, Mr. President. The worst would have been Morgan shooting you from the first-floor window of Gould & Co. when you got out of your car outside Senator Harvey Black's town house to join him for dinner."

"Which invitation I canceled on your advice a week ago. You said then you wished to handle this business yourself. No one from the FBI, no police, no military. Even the head of the Secret Service was excluded, which makes it puzzling that you got away with using Clancy in this affair."

Clancy intruded. "I was served a presidential warrant, Mr. President, so I had to do as I was told."

"I have a stack of them in my safe," Blake said. "All signed by you."

"Really. And you just fill in a name?"

"Correct, Mr. President. You know how the Basement works."

During the Cold War, when it appeared the Communists were infiltrating at every level of government, the then-President had invented the Basement as a small operation answerable only to him. Since then, it had been handed from one President to another. It was one of his most valuable assets. All other agencies were tied up in rules and regulations, the legal system. This was not. The presidential warrant cut through the crap. People thought Johnson was a deskman. In fact, he had a file of names of ex-FBI and Secret Service men he could pull in on an ad hoc basis. He could connect at any time with General Charles Ferguson in London, who ran a similar organization for the British Prime Minister.

"I can, in effect, kill for you," Blake went on. "I can have, for example, someone like Morgan disposed of without a trace, but only if I'm left alone to do things my way. The war on terrorism can't be won unless we're willing to fight back on our own terms. Fight fire with fire."

"And where does that leave the rule of law?"

"I'm not sure. People at Al Qa'eda would have their own answer to that. All I know is that we won't beat them by playing patty-cake."

"Okay, I take your point. Tell me about this Morgan business. You said you didn't want me to know too many details before. Tell me now."

"It was Major Roper who came up with it."

"Yes, I know about him. The bomb-disposal hero who ended up in a wheelchair."

"And made a new career for himself in computers. Anything you want in cyberspace, Roper can find for you, but his great gift is developing new programs in which millions of facts can be overviewed in seconds. Take your evening out with Senator Black. The computer imaged that town house on Park Avenue, the surrounding properties. He then tapped in to every detail about the buildings, what was going on there, the personnel involved, and so on."

At that moment, Millie came in with a tray and the bacon sandwiches. "They smell good enough to eat, Millie. I might have one myself. Eat up, gentlemen, but carry on, Blake. What's so special about what Roper's up to, surely our people can do that?"

"Frankly, not as brilliantly as he can. His programs can show given nationalities, religious backgrounds, family, anything you want, and all at lightning speed. It also indicates anomalies, things that shouldn't be. It means his computer is thinking for itself and making deductions, but doing it at a speed beyond human comprehension."

"Conceptual thought by a machine. Quite something," Cazalet said.

"Anyway, to cut it short, the computer threw up the nationalities of the people working in the area of Black's town house, which were many. Some of them were English, and Roper, interested, cross-referenced the identities, passports, birthplaces and religions, and in no time at all, one Henry Morgan, who'd been working as a security guard at Gould & Co. opposite Black's house, popped up. He was English, but with a Muslim mother."

"Really. Is that unusual?"

"Just enough so that what Roper saw next rang bells: Morgan was a highly qualified pharmacist with a master's degree, who also taught at London University, and he entered our country on a tourist visa."

It was Clancy who put in, "So why does a guy like that take a job as a security guard, Mr. President—and on a forged green card?"

"Something else Roper discovered."

"Everything about us is on some sort of record these days," the President said. "So General Ferguson tipped you off."

"No, there was more to it than that. Ferguson found Roper's discovery interesting enough to check it out a little on his side. He sent his assistant, Detective Superintendent Hannah Bernstein of Special Branch at Scotland Yard, to visit Morgan's home address in London. She discovered that the mother was in a wheelchair after a bad automobile accident that had killed the father five years ago. Bernstein posed as a welfare officer to gain her confidence. Discovered many interesting things."

"Such as?"

"The mother had been disowned by her family for marrying out of the Muslim faith. Her son had been raised a Christian. After the accident, however, she rediscovered her faith and her son would take her to the local mosque, where she was received well. And the truly interesting thing was that she said her son had discovered Islam himself, and embraced it."

Cazalet was looking grim. "So it all begins to fit."

"Especially when she said he'd gone to New York on vacation."

"Has Ferguson taken it any further?"

"No, he's waiting to hear from us."

Cazalet nodded. "So Morgan obviously arrived on somebody's orders."

"Exactly. An organization in the UK with some sort of contacts in New York."

"Why didn't you arrest him the minute you got the story from London?"

"I wanted to see where it would lead, and Charles Ferguson agreed. It was highly unlikely he was just a deranged loner, so there was a chance he could lead us to his New York contacts."

"Only he didn't."

"The few days he was here, he didn't meet a soul. I had two old FBI hands follow him when we found that the address he'd given Icon Security was false. He was staying in a small hotel; they discreetly gained access to his room and found nothing. No ID on him, no passport at his death. I'd say they'd all been destroyed, probably on orders from his handlers in London."

"They obviously were hanging him out to dry."

"Exactly, and the cyanide tooth indicates the equivalent of a suicide bombing. He wasn't meant to survive."

Cazalet said, "Okay, I know there's a lot of supposition here, but I admit it makes a hell of a lot of sense. It still leaves the question of the AK. Where did that come from?"

"It certainly wasn't in his hotel room," Clancy said. "We figure it was probably left in some locker, maybe a train or bus station."

"By his unknown contacts in New York," Blake put in. "By prearrangement. He'd have been given the location, supplied with a key. Again, it's supposition, but I'd say he didn't pick that bag up until he was on his way to work."

"Yes, it makes sense, all of it," Cazalet said. "He would have made an interesting prisoner, but now he's dead, which leaves *us* with a dead end." He frowned. "Except for Ferguson and his people."

"Exactly what I was thinking, Mr. President. Maybe we can find out more from the English end."

"The mother," Cazalet said, "maybe she knows something."

"I don't know. A handicapped, aging lady in a wheelchair is hardly the sort of person that Al Qa'eda would be recruiting," Blake said. "But she and her son were welcomed warmly at the local mosque."

"Which is where we should look." Cazalet nodded. "Ferguson's the man to handle it." He smiled. "It's London next stop for you, Blake. I'll speak to Ferguson myself and promise him every assistance."

"What about me, Mr. President?" Clancy said.

"No way. I need you to watch my back. You took a bullet for me once, Clancy. You're my good-luck charm."

"As you wish, Mr. President."

Blake said, "I'd like to keep a low profile on this one. I'll fly over in one of our private planes, with your permission, and use Farley Field outside London, Ferguson's base for special operations."

"By all means. As soon as you can." He hesitated. "When you asked me to cancel dinner with Senator Black, you didn't tell me much, and I hesitated. Thank God I had enough faith in you."

"Just doing my job, Mr. President."

Blake went and opened the door, and Cazalet called, "And, Blake . . ."

"Mr. President?"

"Take them down. Whoever they are, take them down."

"You can count on it, Mr. President," and Blake went out.

LONDON

3

The Gulfstream came in to Farley Field right on time
and Blake thanked the crew, alighted and walked
across the tarmac, pausing to look around him. A lot
of water under the bridge at this place, and not just the
struggles with the Rashid empire.

A voice called, "Hey, Blake. Over here."

Blake turned and saw a Daimler by the control tower,
parked close to the entrance of the operations room. The
man standing beside it was no more than five feet five,
with hair so fair it was almost white. He wore an old
black leather bomber jacket and jeans, and a cigarette
dangled from the corner of his mouth. The man was
Sean Dillon, once a feared enforcer for the IRA and now
Ferguson's right hand.

Blake shook hands. "How are you, my fine Irish friend?"

"All the better for seeing you. The right royal treatment you're getting, Ferguson sending the Daimler."

They climbed in the back and the chauffeur drove away. Blake said, "So how are things?"

"Pretty warm since Ferguson heard from the President. Jesus, Mary and Joseph, Blake, but that was a close call."

"You know how it is, Sean, you've been there. I remember how you saved President Clinton and Prime Minister Major on that Thames riverboat years back, and took a knife in the back for your trouble."

"From Norah Bell, the original bitch and worse than any man, and it took a decent woman like Hannah Bernstein to shoot her dead."

"How is Hannah?"

"Wonderful, as usual. If she didn't work for Ferguson, I think she'd have been Chief Superintendent by now or even Commander at Scotland Yard."

"But she loves you all too much to move on?"

"Blake, she's still trying to reform the lot of us. You know her grandfather is a rabbi. It's that moral perception of hers. She's been shot to bits, had her life shortened in any number of ways, and still hangs in there trying to keep Ferguson and me in check."

"And fails in that respect." It was a statement, not a question.

Dillon said, "Blake, the world's gone to hell in a

handbasket. Terrorism, Al Qa'eda, all that stuff since nine-eleven, has changed everything. It can't be combated by the old-fashioned rules of war. It isn't like that."

"I agree." Blake shrugged. "A few years ago, I'd never have said that, in spite of what I had to do during my time in Vietnam. I believed in the decencies, the rule of law, justice, all that stuff. But the people we have to deal with these days—there are no rules as far as they're concerned, so there are no rules as far as I'm concerned. I'll take them down any way I can."

"Good man yourself, I couldn't agree more." Dillon lit another cigarette. "I speak Arabic, you know that, and I've spent my share of time in the Middle East. Even worked for the PLO in the old days when I was a naughty boy, and I think I know the Arab mind a bit. Most Muslims in the States or the UK are decent people, interested only in making a living and raising their families, but there's a few of them who have a different political agenda, and it's dealing with them that's the problem."

"Take Morgan. English father, Muslim mother, raised a Christian," Blake said. "I know what happened to his parents, his mother returning to the Islamic faith and Morgan finding that same faith himself. But what turned him into the assassin who tried to take out the President?"

"Well, that's what you're here to find out," Dillon told him. "And Ferguson, Hannah and Roper are waiting at Cavendish Place to discuss it with you."

The Embassy of the Russian Federation is situated in Kensington Palace Gardens and it was typical November weather, rain falling, when Greta Novikova emerged through the main gates and paused at the edge of the pavement, waiting for the traffic to pass.

She was a small girl, unmistakably Slavic, with black hair to her shoulders, dark intense eyes, and high cheekbones, and she wore an ankle-length coat in soft black leather over a black Armani suit. She would have made heads turn anywhere. She was a commercial attaché at the embassy and had the degree to prove it, but in fact, at thirty-five years old she was a major in the GRU, Russian Military Intelligence.

She crossed the road during a break in the traffic and entered the pub opposite. Early lunchtime it wasn't very busy, but the man she was seeking was at the far end of the bar in the window seat reading the London *Times*.

He was a couple of inches short of six feet, and wore a fawn raincoat over a dark wool suit. His hair was close-cropped, and a scar ran from the bottom of his left eye to the corner of his mouth. The eyes were cold and watchful, and the face powerful. The face of a soldier, which in a way he had been. A man of forty-five who had joined the KGB at twenty and had made major when he had moved on to other things. Afghanistan, Chechnya, Iraq in the old days—he'd seen it all. His name was Yuri Ashimov.

He stood up and kissed her on both cheeks and spoke to her in Russian. "Greta, more lovely than usual. A drink?"

"I'll have a vodka with you."

He went to the bar, ordered two, brought them back, sat down, took out a pack of Russian cigarettes and lit one.

"So, as nothing incredibly shocking has happened in New York, you must have a story for me."

"Not a thing," she said.

"Come on, Greta, GRU handles all things Arabic and Muslim. There has to be something."

"That's the point. There isn't. The President didn't keep his damned appointment with Senator Black. After the function at the Pierre, he went straight to Washington."

"And Morgan?"

"Certainly went to Gould & Co. as usual. One of our New York associates confirmed this. The only unusual activity was some sort of paramedic ambulance going down into the underground parking lot. It left half an hour later."

"Did our associate follow?"

"He deemed it unwise."

"I should bloody well think so. It stinks."

"Do you think they got him?"

"Sounds likely. But if they have, they won't let on, and it won't affect us anyway. There were no direct contacts."

Greta nodded. "I think they'd want him alive to see

what he had to say. On the other hand, our American friends are a lot lighter on the trigger these days and he did have the cyanide tooth."

"Alive or dead, they won't advertise the fact. What about the mother?"

"I called yesterday, as you suggested. Brought flowers and a basket of fruit, supposedly from friends at the mosque."

"How was she?"

"Faded—slightly confused as usual. She told me everyone at the mosque was so kind, Dr. Selim was fantastic. And she mentioned that someone from the Council Welfare Department had visited her. A woman, apparently."

Ashimov frowned. "Why would the Welfare Department visit her?"

"Because she's handicapped?"

"Rubbish. Her son's well enough off. Why would Welfare visit?" He shook his head. "I don't like it. Did she say if they would visit again?"

"I don't know."

"Be there, Greta. Just in case. If somebody turns up, I want a photo. I get an instinct for things."

"Which is why you're still here, my love."

"True. But something here isn't right. Let's try and find out what it is."

At Cavendish Place, Dillon and Blake were admitted by Kim, the General's Ghurka manservant, and found

Ferguson, Hannah Bernstein and Roper in the drawing room. Ferguson was in his sixties, a large, untidy man in a crumpled suit and a Guards tie. Hannah Bernstein was in her early thirties, with close-cropped red hair and horn-rimmed spectacles. Her Armani trouser suit was certainly more expensive than most people could afford on police pay. Major Roper sat in a state-of-the-art electric wheelchair, wearing a reefer coat, hair down to his shoulders, his face a taut mask of the kind of scar tissue that comes from burns, the explosion that had ended his career.

"Here he is, the man of the moment," Dillon said. "I'm sure he'll give it to us in graphic detail," which Blake did, everything that had happened in Manhattan.

Afterward, Blake said, "So there it is. For the disposal system, I'm indebted to you, General. We're fighting a new kind of war these days, although I can understand Hannah's moral principles being bruised a bit."

"Bruised or not, the Superintendent works for this department under the Official Secrets Act. Isn't that right?" Ferguson glanced at her.

Hannah didn't look easy, but said, "Of course, sir."

"Good. Tell us about Mrs. Morgan, then."

"She's sixty-five and looks much older. I managed to get hold of her hospital records, and it's bad. The automobile accident that killed her husband almost finished her off. She narrowly avoided being a paraplegic, but she has money. Her husband owned a pharmacy, which was sold after his death, and there was insurance, so she's well-fixed."

"Go on."

"Her family disowned her when she married a Christian, but now she's returned to Islam, as you know. Her son started taking her to the Queen Street Mosque in her wheelchair. It used to be a Methodist chapel."

"And he turned, too?"

"Apparently."

Blake said, "That really interests me, the idea of a highly educated man, ostensibly English for thirty years of his life, a university academic, turning to a faith he'd never accepted before in his life."

"And then ending up in Manhattan with the intention of killing the President," Dillon said.

"Which makes me wonder what goes on at the Queen Street Mosque," Blake said. "Some of these places are hotbeds of intrigue, pump out the wrong ideas. Sure, we finally captured Saddam in Iraq. But how long ago was that and how many terrorist attacks have there been since?"

Ferguson said, "In his last message, Bin Laden spoke of his young extremists as being 'soldiers of God,' and what concerns us is that young men from this country could be among them. It makes places like the Queen Street Mosque of special interest."

Hannah said, "If you're looking for suicide bombers, though, it doesn't seem like the place." She opened a file and passed it across. "Dr. Ali Selim, the imam. Forty-five, born in London, father a doctor from Iraq who sent the boy to St. Paul's School, one of our better establishments. Selim went to Cambridge, studied Arabic, and later took a doctorate in comparative theology."

Blake looked at the file, particularly the photo. "Impressive. I like the beard." He passed the file to the others.

Hannah said, "He's a member of the Muslim Council, the Mayor of London's Interfaith Committee, and any number of government boards. Everyone I speak to tells me he's a wonderful man."

"Maybe he's too wonderful," Dillon said.

"I've checked with the local police. Not a hint of trouble at the Queen Street Mosque."

There was a pause, and Ferguson turned to Roper. "Have you any thoughts, Major?"

"I can only process facts, opinions, suppositions. Unless I have something to go on, I can't help."

"Well, I'll give you something," Blake said. "And it's been intriguing the hell out of me. Does the Wrath of Allah mean anything to you?"

"Should it?"

"When Clancy and I faced Morgan, in the moment before he bit on the cyanide tooth, Morgan said, 'Beware the Wrath of Allah.'"

Roper frowned and shook his head. "It doesn't strike a chord, but I'll run it by my computer."

"So, the way ahead on this one appears plain," Ferguson said. "I think you, Superintendent, should have another word with Mrs. Morgan in your guise as a welfare worker."

Hannah wasn't comfortable and showed it. "That's a

difficult one, sir. I mean, her son is dead and she doesn't even know it."

"Which can't be helped, Superintendent. It's an unusual situation, I agree, but when one considers the gravity of the deed Morgan was trying to commit, I feel that any means that will help us to reach an explanation would be justified. See to it, and use Dillon as backup. His knowledge of Arabic may prove useful." He turned to Blake. "We'll drop Roper off at his house, and you and I can continue to the Ministry of Defence, where I'll show you everything we have on Muslim activity in the UK."

"Suits me fine," Blake said.

Ferguson turned to the others. "All right, people, there's work to be done, let's get to it."

After leaving the pub on Kensington High Street, Greta and Ashimov crossed the road to the embassy and got into a dark blue Opel sedan. She checked the glove compartment and found a digital camera.

"Excellent," he told her. "You can drop me at my apartment in Monk Street and keep in touch on your mobile. Anything of significance, I want to know."

"Of course." She drove out into the traffic. "Where's Belov at the moment?"

"The good Josef is in Geneva. All those billions, my love, it keeps him so busy." There was an edge of bitterness there.

"Come off it," she said. "Money is power and you

love it, andworking for Josef Belov is the ultimate power and you love that too."

"To a point—only to a point." She turned into Monk Street and stopped. He said, "Sometimes I think it was better in the old days, Greta. Afghanistan, Chechnya, Iraq. To smell powder again." He shook his head. "That would be wonderful."

"You must be raving mad," she told him.

"Very probably." He patted her silken knee. "You're a lovely girl, so go and do what Belov is paying you to do. Extract a few more facts from Mrs. Morgan, but keep your masters at the GRU happy."

He got out of the Opel and walked away.

Heavy traffic on Wapping High Street held her back a little, but she finally found what she was looking for: Chandler Street, backing down to the Thames. Many cars were parked there, which gave her good cover, and she pulled in, switched off and settled down, her camera at the ready.

Number thirteen. That had amused her when she'd looked at the file, an old Victorian terrace house. She sat there, looking along the street to the grocery shop on the corner opposite the river. There was no one about, not a soul. It started to rain, and then a red Mini car drew up opposite and Hannah Bernstein and Sean Dillon got out.

Hannah pressed the bell push and they waited. Finally, they heard the sounds of movement, the door was opened on a chain and Mrs. Morgan peered out. She was old, faded, much older than her years, as Hannah had indicated. She had a long scarf wrapped around her head, the chador worn by most Muslim women. The voice was almost a whisper.

"What do you want?"

"It's me, Mrs. Morgan, Miss Bernstein from the Welfare Department. I thought I'd call again."

"Oh, yes."

"This is Mr. Dillon, my supervisor. May we come in?"

"Just a moment." The door closed while she disengaged the chain, then opened again. When they entered, she had turned to precede them in the wheelchair.

All this, Greta Novikova had captured on her camera.

In the small sitting room, the air was heavy and close and smelled of musk, a strange, disturbing aroma that was somehow alien and not quite right.

Hannah said, "I just thought I'd check on you, Mrs. Morgan, as we happened to be passing."

Dillon, more direct, said, "Your son is in New York, I understand, Mrs. Morgan. Have you heard from him?"

Her voice was muted, and she coughed. "Oh, he'll be too busy. I'm sure he'll phone when he's got time."

Hannah was angry and glared at Dillon. He nodded, and she carried on reluctantly. "Have you seen Dr. Selim lately?"

"Oh, yes, at the mosque. When my son's away, Dr. Selim sends a young man to wheel me along to Queen Street. It's not far. He's been very good, Dr. Selim, helping us so much, helping me and my Henry, to discover our faith."

Hannah felt wretched. "I'm sure that's been very nice for you."

"Yes, he's called round two or three times since Henry's been away with his friend."

There was a pause, her breathing heavy. Dillon said, "And who was that?"

"Oh, I can't remember his name. Very strange, Russian, I think. He had a terrible scar right down from his eye to the corner of his mouth."

Dillon said sternly in Arabic, "Have you told me everything, old woman? Do you swear to this, as Allah commands?"

She looked fearful and replied in Arabic, "There is no more. I don't know his name. My son said he was a Russian friend. That's all I know."

Hannah said, "I don't know what you're saying, Dillon, but leave it. She's frightened."

Dillon smiled, suddenly looking devastatingly charming, and kissed Mrs. Morgan on the forehead. "There you are, my love." He turned to Hannah and led the way out.

Outside, she said, "What a bastard you are. What were you saying?"

"Just checking if she was telling the truth."

"Right, let's go."

"I'm not ready yet, Hannah." He nodded to the corner shop at the end of the street. "Let's have a word down there. The Russian gentleman with the scar interests me. Maybe he's been in."

They walked down the pavement toward the shop, and behind them, Greta Novikova turned her Opel into the street and drove away.

The sign on the shop window said M. PATEL. Dillon nodded. "Indian, that's good."

"Why, particularly?" Hannah asked.

"Because they're smart and they don't screw around. They've got a head for business and they want to fit in. So let's see what Mr. Patel has to say and let's use your warrant card."

The shop was neat and orderly, and obviously sold a bit of everything. The Indian behind the counter reading the *Evening Standard* was in shirtsleeves and looked about fifty. He glanced up, smiling, looked them over and stopped smiling.

"Can I help?"

Hannah produced her warrant card. "Detective Superintendent Bernstein, Special Branch. Mr. Dillon is a colleague. We're pursuing inquiries, which involve a Mrs. Morgan who lives up the street. You know her?"

"Of course I do."

"Her son's away," Dillon said. "New York, I understand?"

"Yes, she did tell me that. Look, what is this?"

"Don't fret, Mr. Patel, everything's fine. Mrs. Morgan is friendly with a Dr. Ali Selim. You know who he is?"

Patel's face slipped. "Yes, I do."

"And don't like him." Dillon smiled. "A Hindu-Muslim thing? Well, never mind. Sometimes when he sees Mrs.

Morgan, he has a friend with him. Bad scar, from his eye to his mouth. She thinks he's Russian."

"That's right, he is. He's called in to buy cigarettes, sometimes with the Arab. Selim calls him Yuri. They were in yesterday."

Hannah glanced up at the security camera. "Was that working?"

He nodded. "I was busy, so when the tape stopped, I didn't run it back. I took it out and put a fresh tape in."

"Good," Dillon said. "I'm sure you have a television in the back room. Get us the tape and we'll run it back."

Patel proved accommodating; he closed the shop for a while and ran the tape through for them. Finally he stopped.

"There they are."

Hannah and Dillon had a look. "So that's him?" Dillon said. "The Russian."

"Yes. And I've remembered something else," Patel said. "One day, he was on his own and his mobile rang and he said, 'Ashimov here.'"

"You're sure about that?" Hannah asked.

"Well, that's how it sounded."

"Good man, yourself," Dillon said. "You've helped enormously."

Patel hesitated. "Look, is Mrs. Morgan in trouble? I mean, she's not fit to be out, but she's nice enough."

"No problem," Hannah said. "We're just pursuing some inquiries."

"And I know exactly what that means with you people."

Dillon patted him on the shoulder. "Don't worry, old son, we're the good guys."

They went out and walked toward the Mini. "Yuri Ashimov," Hannah said. "Interesting."

"Let's go and see what Roper makes of it," Dillon told her.

At Monk Street, Greta linked her digital camera to Ashimov's television and ran the photos of Dillon and Hannah.

"There you are. The Welfare officer, I assume. I've no idea who the man is."

Ashimov swore softly. "But I do. My God, Greta, you're onto something here."

"What on earth do you mean?"

"Last year, when Baron von Berger of Berger International was killed in that plane crash, and Belov took over his oil concessions and put me in charge of general security . . . I started going over all of Berger International's previous security records. Did you know that Berger was in a state of open warfare against a man named General Charles Ferguson? Have you heard of him?"

"Of course I have," Greta said. "He runs that special intelligence outfit for the Prime Minister."

"Gold star for you, Greta." Ashimov pointed to the last picture on the screen. "That's Detective Superintendent Hannah Bernstein, Ferguson's assistant."

"Good God," Greta said.

Ashimov flicked to Dillon. "And this gentleman—

this one really is special. Sean Dillon, Ferguson's strong right hand, and once the Provisional IRA's top enforcer. For twenty years or more, the British Army and the RUC couldn't lay a hand on him."

"And now he works for the Prime Minister? That's unbelievable."

"Well, it's typically British. They'll turn their hands to anything if it suits."

"So where does this leave us?"

"With Ferguson's outfit checking Mrs. Morgan, whose son was supposed to have a go at President Jake Cazalet in New York and has now disappeared, or so it would seem. Would you say the appearance of Dillon and Bernstein at her front door was a coincidence?"

"Not for a moment. What do you intend to do?"

"I'll alert Dr. Ali Selim, naturally. We'll take it from there. I'll show them the photos."

"And Belov?"

"He left this sort of thing in my hands, but I keep him informed." He smiled. "He's not involved, Greta my love, you must understand. He's too important. As regards operations at what you might call the coal face, I'm in charge." He smiled and kissed her on the cheek. "Trust me."

Soon after, he was standing by an old jetty around the corner from the Queen Street Mosque, overlooking the river. He leaned on a rail smoking a cigarette, enjoying the landscape, the views, the boats passing. Selim appeared after a while, a handsome bearded man wearing a Burberry raincoat, an umbrella guarding him from the rain.

"Yuri, my friend." He smiled. "You said it was urgent. Why not call at my office at the mosque?"

"Not again," Ashimov told him. "I've got news for you. Our friend Morgan's trip to New York would seem to have disappeared into a black hole."

"How unfortunate," Selim said calmly.

"Listen." Ashimov went through everything.

Afterward, Selim said, "We can't be certain he met a bad end. That's supposition, surely?"

"Ali, my friend, if Ferguson's lot are involved, particularly this Dillon, then the end is as certain as the coffin lid closing."

"You consider the man exceptional, it would seem."

"And for good reason. He's a man of many skills. An experienced pilot, for instance, and linguist. Russian and Arabic, for example."

"I'll remember that."

"Besides his years with the IRA, he worked for the PLO as a mercenary, and for the Israelis in Lebanon in the old days." Ashimov lit a cigarette. "He kills at the drop of a hat, this one."

"Oh, in a dark street on a rainy night, I'm sure he's as susceptible to a knife under the ribs as anyone."

"My dear Ali." Ashimov smiled. "If you believe that, you'll be making the worst mistake of your life."

Selim said, "So what about Mrs. Morgan? If they're

sniffing around there, she could be saying the wrong things."

"I don't know. She's an aging cripple in a wheelchair. She can't speak in much more than a whisper. And what could she tell him? That she's a woman who returned to Islam after her husband's death, whose son also discovered the faith and lightened her grief. Wouldn't you, as her imam, agree with all this?"

"Of course."

"Exactly, and you are a man of impeccable background and highly respected. Whatever has happened to the son has no connection with you. You're too important, Ali, that's why we keep you out of it. You even sat on a committee at the House of Commons last week. Nothing could be more respectable. No, my friend, you're a real asset."

"And too valuable to lose," Selim said. "And loose ends are loose ends. If Mrs. Morgan should happen to mention you and me in the same breath, they'll discover who you are. The man who is Belov's security."

Ashimov sighed. "All right, leave it to me. Now we better split up. I'll be in touch."

Selim hesitated. "Morgan was a soldier of God. If worse has come to the worst, he is also a true martyr."

"Save that tripe for the young fools at the mosque, your Wrath of Allah fanatics. Go on, get going."

Selim went, and Ashimov stayed there thinking about it. Perhaps Selim had a point. After all, why would Bernstein and Dillon be calling on the old lady at all? Better to be safe than sorry. He looked over at the incoming tide, then pulled up his collar against the rain, walked around to Chandler Street and rang the bell at number thirteen.

She answered it after a while and peered out over the chain. "It's me. Mr. Ashimov," he said. "Dr. Selim's friend. He asked me to call and see if you wanted to go to the mosque."

"That is kind," she said. "I was going to go a little later."

"Since I'm here, why don't you go now? It's much easier if I push you," he said. "Bring an umbrella. It's raining."

She closed the door, undid the chain and opened it again and Ashimov stepped in. "Let me help you." He reached for a raincoat and a beret hanging on a hall stand and helped her. "There you are, and here's an umbrella." He took one down and gave it to her.

"So kind," she said.

"Not at all. Have you got your key?"

"Yes."

"You had a visit this afternoon, I believe. A lady from the Welfare Department?"

"Did I?" She frowned. "I can't remember."

"Yes, with a gentleman. What did they ask you? About your son in New York?"

She was confused and bewildered. Few things seemed real to her anymore, and her memory was fading fast these days.

"I can't remember. I can't remember anyone calling."

Which was true, for she was in the early stages of Alzheimer's. It was obvious to Ashimov that he was wasting his time.

"Never mind. Let's be on our way, then."

The rain was driving down, no one around as they went along the street, the fog drifting up from the river. They went past the shop, which now showed a closed sign inside the door.

"It's going to be a dirty night later," he said.

"I think you're right."

"But still a nice view of the Thames." He turned in at the old wooden jetty, the wheels of her chair trembling over the warped wooden boarding.

"There you are." He paused at the top of the steps going down to the river.

"I like it at night with the lights on the boats."

Her voice was like a small wind through the trees on a dark evening, as he looked at the river high with water lapping at the bottom of the steps. Then he shoved the chair forward. Strangely enough, she didn't call out, but gripped the arms of her chair tightly, and when she hit the water, she went under instantly as the chair emptied her out.

It was only four or five feet deep, a mud bank when the tide was out. Someone would find her soon enough. He'd done her a favor, really. He lit a cigarette and walked away.

A few minutes later, standing in a doorway, he phoned Ali Selim. "You can relax. Mrs. Morgan has met with an unfortunate accident."

"What are you talking about?" Ashimov told him. Selim sounded horrified. "Was that necessary?"

"Come on, Selim, you were the one talking about loose ends. Now, don't forget, if the police inquire, you were unhappy about her habit of going to the mosque alone in her wheelchair, which is why you often sent young men to fetch her."

Selim took a deep breath. "Of course."

"She was prematurely aging, confused a great deal of the time."

"She had Alzheimer's."

"Well, there you are. I'll leave it with you," and Ashimov hung up.

4

It was at ten the following morning that Patel, exercising his small terrier, found the body and the wheelchair on the beach. He called the Wapping police, and since Hannah had put a tracer on Mrs. Morgan, she was notified at once at the Ministry of Defence.

Ferguson was in a Defence Committee meeting, but Dillon was in the office and she quickly filled him in.

"So what do we do?" he demanded.

"Get down to Chandler Street fast and I'll put a red flag on the case and take command. You come with me. You might be useful."

They used a department limousine with a civilian driver, retired police. Hannah said, "It's one hell of a coincidence."

"And you know how much I believe in those."

Just then, Dillon's mobile rang. "Sean? It's Roper. I've got something interesting for you on Ashimov and also on the Wrath of Allah thing."

"Hold on to it for just a bit. Mrs. Morgan's turned up on a mudflat at the end of her street, and Hannah and I are on our way. We're just about there. I'll call you later."

They took a turn, and then there they were. There was a police paramedic's ambulance, the usual team, and a sergeant in charge who jumped to attention when Hannah showed him her warrant card and assumed command.

"Not much of a scene of crime, ma'am," he said. "Plenty of mud." She and Dillon looked over the rail. "It's obvious what happened. The gent who found her said she was always pushing herself in her wheelchair up and down the street to the Queen Street Mosque. Come off the pavement twice before in the past and ended up in the gutter."

Hannah said, "Right. Get her up out of there and deliver her to Peel Street Morgue. I'm going to call in Professor George Langley. He'll handle it."

She walked away with her mobile and stood in a doorway. Dillon saw Patel lurking outside his shop and went over.

"This must have been a shock for you?"

"A terrible shock. It was a higher tide than usual last night. It's amazing she wasn't swept away."

"Are you surprised by what happened?"

"Not really. She'd had a few close calls in that wheelchair and she was worse these days."

"What do you mean, worse?"

"Couldn't handle herself, confused, no memory worth speaking of. She didn't know which way she was pointing. She was very upset when Henry went off to the States." Patel hesitated. "What was it all about before, you and the Superintendent and those inquiries?"

Dillon lied glibly. "Her son was only on a special tourist visa, but seems to have gone missing, and we had a request to check it out. A lot of people do that. Go as tourists and fade into the landscape."

"A lot of people do that here, too," Patel said.

"The way of the world."

Dillon went over to Hannah as she finished her call. "What next?"

"I've spoken to Langley, and he's going straight to the morgue." A couple of paramedics carried Mrs. Morgan past them in a body bag. "Poor old lady," Hannah said.

"And nothing we can do. But speaking of doing things, Roper seems to have come up with some stuff about Ashimov and the Wrath of Allah thing."

"Good. I'll speak to the General," which she did briefly and turned to Dillon. "He suggests we all meet up at Roper's apartment, get filled in together."

"Sounds good to me." He shook his head. "I accept everything Patel says about Mrs. Morgan and her wheelchair, about her incompetence and so on, her minor accidents—but it doesn't explain what she was doing on the jetty in the first place."

"Exactly what I was thinking."

Roper's apartment was on the ground floor, with a ramp entrance to facilitate his wheelchair. The entire place was designed for not only a handicapped person, but one determined to look after himself. His equipment was state-of-the-art, some of it top secret and supplied by Ferguson.

Dillon and Hannah had been with him for perhaps ten minutes when Ferguson arrived and joined them.

"So where are we?" he asked Hannah. "With Mrs. Morgan, I mean."

"I've pulled in Professor Langley, sir. He's working on her now."

"He won't find much, not in my opinion." Dillon told Ferguson all Patel had said. "So there you are. It's highly suspicious, but I doubt we can prove it's any more than an accident."

Ferguson looked gloomy. "One thing's certain. We can't throw the fact that Henry Morgan is dead into the pot, because we're not supposed to know. So where does that leave us?"

"With Yuri Ashimov, for one thing," Roper said. "Formerly the pride of the KGB." He punched his computer keys and Ashimov's photo emerged. One or two in uniform, others in a more social situation.

"What's he up to now?"

"Head of security for Josef Belov and his outfit."

"The oil billionaire?" Dillon asked.

"That's the man," Roper said. "Man of mystery, that's

his front. A billionaire many times over, and friend of Putin."

"So what on earth would Ashimov be doing around Mrs. Morgan?"

"It must have been something to do with the son," Hannah said. "Has to be."

"And the interesting question is Who sent Henry Morgan to New York with the intention of shooting the President?" Dillon turned to Hannah. "You said Dr. Ali Selim was clean as a whistle."

It was Roper who broke in. "He is, as far as my researches show."

"Then why is he involved with a man like Ashimov? What's the purpose?" Dillon shook his head. "There has to be a reason." He turned to Roper. "What did you find out about the Wrath of Allah?"

"It was an Arab militant group some years ago during the civil war in Lebanon. With the end of that war, it seemed to disappear from view. Last year, the Israeli Mossad tried to establish if it was an offshoot of Al Qa'eda, but got nowhere.

"Well, it meant something to Henry Morgan," Ferguson said. "It may have disappeared, but that doesn't mean it doesn't exist. One of our greatest security problems is the way a few terrorists can hide themselves in the mass of an ordinary decent Muslim population. How can you tell the difference?"

"Mao Tse-tung invented that strategy years ago, and it eventually won him China," Dillon pointed out.

"I've got something else for you, recently pulled out

of my printer." Roper handed three photos across. "Greta Novikova. Supposed to be a secretary at the Russian Embassy, but in reality a major in the GRU. Used to be Ashimov's girlfriend. Neat coincidence, her being assigned to London, isn't it?"

"Quite a lady," Dillon said admiringly. He slipped a copy into his breast pocket. "Maybe I'll run into her."

Hannah's mobile went, she answered and listened. "Fine, we'll be there." She turned to Ferguson. "Professor Langley, sir. He can give us a preliminary."

"Excellent," Ferguson said. "You hang in there, Major. I'll keep you informed."

They filed into Ferguson's Daimler, and as it moved away, Greta Novikova eased out in her Opel and went after them.

George Langley was a small, gray-haired energetic man whom they had all met in the pursuance of previous cases. Many people considered him the greatest forensic pathologist in London, and not much escaped him.

The Peel Street Morgue was an old building, some of it Victorian, but the interior was modern enough. A receptionist led them into a white-tiled room with fluorescent lighting and modern steel operating tables. Mrs. Morgan lay on one of them. The wounds from her examination had been stitched up.

"My God, I never get used to this part," Hannah said softly.

Langley came in from the preparation room in shirt-sleeves, drying his hands on a towel.

"Ah, there you are, Charles."

"Good of you to be so quick off the mark, George. What have you got for me?"

"Death by drowning. No suggestion of foul play. Strangely enough, no bruising. On the other hand, she was as light as a feather. Very undernourished. Her previous medical history isn't good. The car accident, which reduced her to the wheelchair, was very grave. I've checked the records. I've also checked with her GP, and she was being treated for Alzheimer's."

"So that's it?"

"I'd say so. It's interesting that the man who found her, Patel, speaks of these minor accidents she suffered in the wheelchair. I notice a report by the scene-of-crime sergeant who went to see the imam at Queen Street. Sounded most distressed, said he'd implored her many times not to venture out alone, and usually sent someone to escort her."

"Which still leaves us wondering what she was doing at the end of the jetty," Dillon said.

"I've had a quick look. Nothing out of the ordinary. The Alzheimer's would make her subject to confusion, memory loss, considerable general stress. If she turned right, she'd turn the corner for the Queen Street Mosque; if she turned left, she'd find herself on the jetty and only a few yards to the steps." He didn't even frown when he said, "Are you looking for suspicious circumstances here, Charles? You usually are."

"No, no. It's an unrelated matter."

"Unrelated, huh? Which brings you hotfoot, plus the Superintendent and Dillon? Highly unlikely, I'd have thought. However, I can't help you with this one and I've other things to do. I'll be on my way."

They left and walked to the Daimler. Ferguson paused, frowning, and said to Dillon, "What's that you usually say? About making it a we-know-that-they-know-and-they-know-that-we-know situation?"

"I'd say you mean you want Dr. Ali Selim pushed a little."

"Exactly. I'll leave it to you. Blake's at the American Embassy at the moment. We'll all catch up later."

"Don't you think I should provide a police presence for Selim, sir?" Hannah asked.

"No. Some things require the Dillon touch, Superintendent."

They got in and drove away. Dillon said, "You've noticed the Opel sedan trailing us?"

"Absolutely. Don't forget to find out who it is."

Ferguson dropped him off. Hannah was not pleased, and Dillon leaned down to her through the open window. "Keep the faith, love."

"Well, you keep your fists in your pockets."

The rain increased, and Dillon glanced at the Opel and decided to leave it alone. He went inside the mosque and followed a sign that said OFFICE.

In the Opel, Greta Novikova called Ashimov on his

mobile. "They were all at this Major Roper's place in Regency Square—Ferguson, Bernstein and Dillon. They've now dropped Dillon at Queen Street. Why?"

"I should imagine because Mrs. Morgan has met an untimely accident and Mr. Dillon is about to speak to Selim about it."

"What do you mean, accident?"

"Her wheelchair appears to have deposited her in the Thames. These things happen. Stay there and follow Dillon when he comes out."

Dillon found the office, knocked and walked in. There was no one at reception, so he tried the next door and found his quarry working at a desk.

"Dr. Ali Selim?"

Selim recognized him at once from a computer photo Ashimov had left him.

He managed a smile. "Can I help?"

Dillon decided to let it all hang out. "Oh, I think so, me ould son." He lit a cigarette.

"Not in here. It is an affront," Selim told him.

"I know, a terrible vice, but we all have them. I can see you know who I am, your face twitched, but then a guy like Ashimov would be right on the ball about me and my friends. We have a video of the two of you, by the way. That would go down big at the House of Commons, don't you think? And I notice his girlfriend, Greta Novikova, is outside."

"I don't know what you're talking about."

"Well, in broad terms you do, and I could fill in the rest for you. Henry Morgan walks up a Manhattan street in the rain and disappears into oblivion, his mother goes off the jetty in Chandler Street and into the Thames. A very unfortunate family."

Selim's face turned pale.

"Get out of here. I'll call the police."

"Oh, I don't think you will, not with Ashimov on your back." Dillon dropped his cigarette in a half-filled cup of coffee by Selim's right hand. "Say your prayers, son, you're going to need them. Oh, and good luck with the Wrath of Allah."

It was a long shot, but the shock on Selim's face was obvious.

Dillon went out and paused on the pavement, looking across. Greta Novikova was taking a photo, and she was badly caught out when he crossed the street quickly, opened the passenger door and got in.

"Now, look here . . . ," she started to say.

"Oh, cut it out, girl dear. I know who you are and you know who I am." He produced a packet of Marlboros and took two out. "I bet you smoke, too. Most Russians do."

"Bastard," she said. But she almost looked amused.

He lit the cigarettes and passed her one. "Let's go."

"Go? Where to exactly?"

"My place in Stable Mews. Don't pretend you don't know where that is."

She drove away, half smiling. "I bet Selim was messing himself in there."

"Something like that. I told him we know about Ashimov and you, and who knows? Perhaps Ashimov's boss, the mysterious Josef Belov."

"You're playing with fire, Dillon," she said. "I'd be very careful."

"Oh, I always am."

She paused at the end of Stable Mews. "Can I go now?"

"Of course—unless you'd like to have dinner with me."

"The great Sean Dillon with a romantic side? I doubt it. Besides, you've chosen a bad night. I have a function at the Dorchester ballroom this evening on behalf of the Russian Embassy."

Dillon got out and leaned in. "Oh, I'm sure I could gain admission."

She drove back to the embassy, turning over this strange man in her mind, and phoned Ashimov to tell him what had happened. "I've got a crazy idea he could turn up tonight."

"So he's challenging us, is he? Well, we'll challenge back. I'll go with you. Pick me up at seven."

After she hung up, she went into her computer, into her secret GRU files, accessed Dillon and was breathless at what she discovered. *This* was the man who'd been responsible for the mortar bomb attack on Downing Street in ninety-one? A feared enforcer for the IRA for years, a killer many times over . . . once an *actor* at the *National Theatre*? She read, fascinated.

I put the fear of God into Selim," Dillon told Ferguson on the phone.

"I thought you would. What's your verdict?"

"Well, the obvious thing is that he didn't deny any of it—Morgan, Ashimov, the Novikova woman, the lot."

"Well, he wouldn't, would he? By the way, Blake's been in touch. He's taken all that stuff I gave him on the Muslim situation in the UK and gone straight back to Washington."

"What a shame. I'd hoped to take him to the Dorchester tonight. The Russian Embassy's got a function on in the ballroom. Get me a security pass, Charles, Novikova's going to be there. Perhaps Ashimov will be with her. I'd like to run with it."

"Only if you run with me, you rogue. We'll go together."

"Cocktails at seven, Charles, not black tie. The embassy's trying to make friends and influence people—and I understand that there might be a surprise guest or two."

"Are you referring to the fact that when President Putin finished at the European Union's Paris conference this morning, he decided to divert his plane to RAF Northolt for a chat with the Prime Minister this afternoon? And that he's not due to depart until late tonight?"

"And how would you be knowing that?"

"Because I've been notified of his flight plan out of Northolt to Moscow. It's what they pay me for, dear boy."

"So I'll meet you there?"

"And the Superintendent, too, I think. Dress things up a little. And do me a favor."

"Yours to command."

"Wear one of your better suits. We mustn't let the side down. This should be interesting. I knew Putin rather well in the bad old days, you know, when he was a colonel in the KGB."

"I bet you exchanged shots across the Berlin Wall."

"Something like that. Meet us at the Dorchester as you say, at seven."

"Wouldn't miss it."

In the ballroom at the Dorchester, the great and the good mingled with politicians and civil servants, and waiters passed through the crowd with trays loaded with vodka and the finest champagne, as the Russian Embassy did its best to impress. Yuri Ashimov and Greta stood by a pillar, drinking iced vodka.

"It'll be a hell of a shock for these people when Putin appears with the Prime Minister," Greta said.

"It'll be an even bigger one for you when Belov appears."

"Belov?" She was bewildered. "But why?"

"Because Putin wanted him. Out of all the oil magnates, Josef, my love, is the one the President trusts. They go back a long way." He reached for another vodka as a waiter passed. "I spoke to him a couple of hours ago. Brought him up to speed on the Henry Morgan affair."

"Does Putin know about that?"

"Of course not. There are limits. Josef was philosophical about it, but he wasn't happy about Ferguson and his friends."

"What do we do if Dillon turns up?"

"I hope he does. I have a friend named Harker, Charlie Harker. A crook of the first water, dabbles in everything from protection to drugs to women. Such people have their uses."

"What's he going to do?"

"I mentioned Dillon and gave him a photo. Harker has arranged for two or three of his men to, shall we say, pay special attention to him if he does show up."

Greta said, "I've checked on Dillon, Yuri. He's hell on wheels."

"Well, so am I, my love."

"But it isn't you who'll be doing it. That's what worries me."

"Well, we'll just have to see what happens. Because there he is."

At the same moment, a voice echoed over a microphone as the Russian ambassador called for attention.

"My lords, ladies and gentlemen. I had intended a few words at this moment, but someone far more important has arrived—and with a very special guest."

He gestured and, through the side door, President Putin appeared, the British Prime Minister at his side. The crowd broke into spontaneous applause. The two men stopped for a moment, acknowledging the crowd, then moved on, pausing to shake hands here and there. They were followed by several men, obviously security, but not all.

"The man on the left," Ferguson said. "Black suit, steel-rimmed glasses, cropped hair. Josef Belov. Now, what's he up to?"

Belov looked to be around sixty, his face very calm, giving nothing away. Putin paused for a moment and listened as Belov whispered, "The man standing over there with the woman and the small man with very fair hair, his name is Ferguson. He runs the Prime Minister's private intelligence outfit."

"I know very well who he is, we're old adversaries from the Cold War. What is he to you?"

"No friend."

"Josef," Putin said, "I don't know what you get up to these days and I don't want to know. You are useful to the State. Your billions, and your importance to the oil industry from Iraq to southern Arabia, speaks for itself. However, no one is indispensable, so I'd advise you to be discreet."

"Of course, Mr. President."

Belov faded away and Putin moved on, the crowd parting. He reached Ferguson and smiled.

"It's good to meet old friends. *General* Ferguson now. I like that. You at last outrank me."

"I believe so, Colonel."

Putin smiled and held out his hand, which Ferguson took. "I'm glad you remembered."

"That we swapped shots?"

Putin shrugged. "A long time ago."

"Yes, sir."

Putin turned to walk away, then paused and turned back, his face enigmatic. "And Charles?"

"Sir?"

"I'd take care if I were you—great care."

"Oh, I will, sir, you may depend on it."

Putin moved on.

Hannah said, "What was all that about, sir? It was as if he was warning you."

"Yes, Superintendent. I do believe he was. Now where's Belov gone?"

"Over by the bar with Ashimov and Greta Novikova," Dillon pointed out.

"Well, let's join them." Ferguson smiled. "Could be interesting."

They're coming," Ashimov said. "Perhaps you'd better go."

"Why on earth should I?" Belov said. "This champagne is so good, I'd like another glass. Don't let's pretend with them. I doubt if they will." He turned and smiled. "General Ferguson. A long-overdue pleasure."

"Oh, I doubt that," Ferguson said. "I think you know who my friends are, I certainly know yours." He nodded to Greta. "A pleasure, Major," took her hand and kissed it. "Mind you, the GRU always had style." He turned to Ashimov. "Unlike the KGB."

Ashimov didn't react, and it was Belov who said, "Which would include me, General. There is an English phrase about people in glass houses throwing stones, isn't there? Especially when you have a man like Mr. Dillon at your side, although you, Superintendent, are a credit to Scotland Yard." He emptied his glass, toasting her. "Shall we all have another?"

"An excellent idea," Ferguson said. "I see we have no secrets."

"Especially about you," Dillon said. "And especially about Henry Morgan in Manhattan, and his mother's unfortunate accident." A waiter passed, and they all took glasses of champagne from his tray. "The only thing that confuses me is what one of the richest men in the world would be doing with a bruiser like Ashimov here and a loser like Ali Selim."

"Ah, you don't understand the bigger picture, Dillon," Ferguson said. "Money isn't everything. You're a good case in point. You're rich, but—"

"But he likes to play the game," Belov said.

"Exactly. Being wealthy is like having everything and nothing at the same time, and a man needs more. I remember interrogating a man named Luhzkov years ago. He lectured in economics at London University. A deep-cover agent for the KGB. He often spoke with sincere admiration of a Colonel Belov who headed Department

Three of the KGB. Belov's main task was to create chaos in the Western world—chaos, fear and uncertainty, until the cracks showed and governments toppled."

Belov seemed to stay very calm, though his lips tightened, as did his grip on the champagne glass, and it was Dillon who said, "Just as in Iraq." He shook his head. "All those wonderful oil fields up for grabs, and since Saddam ended up in a cell, who knows where they'll end up?"

Belov put his glass on the bar. "I've heard enough stupidity for one evening. We'll be moving on."

He nodded to Ashimov and Greta and walked away, moving out through the entrance and pausing. Ashimov waved for the limousine.

"I'm sorry, Josef."

"Then do something about it. I have hugely important matters in hand. Our future in Iraq and southern Arabia are on the line. Where Ferguson and his people are concerned, I give you a free hand."

"I've something special lined up for Dillon tonight."

"Good. Just get on with it." Ashimov held the door open for him. Belov got in and put the window down. "I'll be at the Rashid house on South Audley Street for the next three days, then I'm flying to the castle."

"And then Iraq?"

"No, Moscow. I've got to keep the President on our side."

The limousine drove away, and Greta said, "The castle?"

"Drumore Place. It's in County Louth in the Irish Republic. His latest acquisition. A couple of hundred acres, and whatever you want a castle to be, that's what it is. One advantage for him is that the area is a hotbed of Irish nationalism. In that area, the IRA has no idea that the war is over, especially the local commander, one Dermot Kelly."

"Isn't that a problem?"

"For Josef with all his wealth? For a man with no love of the British? The locals have embraced him like one of their own. He goes back a long way with Kelly."

"And you? Do they embrace you as well?"

"Of course. My natural charm."

She smiled. "Now what?"

"I'll give you a nice dinner."

"And Dillon?"

"Oh, he'll be well taken care of." He waved for a passing taxi.

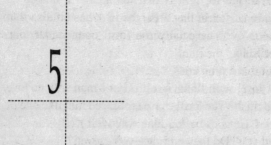

5

At the bar at the Dorchester Ballroom, they were finishing the champagne. Hannah said, "You were a bit heavy, sir."

"Oh, I intended to be. Luhzkov hung himself. Now we all know where we are, which is how I prefer it."

"You ould devil. What you're looking for is a reaction," Dillon said.

"Something like that. I spoke to Roper earlier. Told him to compute a report on Belov. Everything there is. I expect you two to read it thoroughly."

"Of course, sir," Hannah said.

"Good. On our way, then."

They paused at the cloakroom to get coats, and it had started to rain slightly when they went out on the pavement and the Daimler coasted in.

"I'll drop you off," Ferguson said.

"Not me, if you don't mind," Dillon told him. "I feel like the walk."

"In the rain, dear boy?" Ferguson opened the door for Hannah. "You'll have to excuse him, Superintendent. It's an Irish thing, the rain."

"Sure, and your sainted mother, being a Cork woman, would have agreed with you."

"Take care, you rogue, and stay out of trouble."

"Always do, General."

Dillon watched the Daimler drive off, then walked away, his collar up against the rain. He went across the entrance of the hotel and made his way down through Mayfair in the general direction of Shepherd's Market.

That he was being followed had been obvious since leaving the ballroom. Two men, one in a reefer coat and knitted cap, the other in an anorak and baseball cap. Stupid, really, and they'd stuck out like a sore thumb among the kind of people leaving the Dorchester.

Just before reaching Shepherd's Market, he paused on a corner to light a cigarette, then turned into a narrow side street of old town houses, fronted by Victorian spiked railings, with steps leading down to basement areas. He quickened his pace, then dashed down a flight of steps and waited in the darkness.

There was a sound of running steps. A voice said, "Where's he gone, for Christ's sake?"

Dillon came up the steps and stood behind them, hands in the pockets of his raincoat.

"So there you are, lads," he said. "I was beginning to give up on you."

"Why, you little squirt." The man in the reefer coat turned to his friend. "Leave this to me."

He took a length of lead pipe from one pocket. Dillon said, "Very old-fashioned."

"Is that so?"

The man made a sudden rush, arm raised to strike down. Dillon swayed to one side, stamped against the side of one of the man's knees so that he lurched past him, head down, and Dillon put a foot to his backside and sent him headfirst down the steps to the basement.

The man in the baseball cap took a knife from his pocket and sprang the blade. "You little bastard, I'll show you."

"Well, let's be having you, then."

The knife swung, Dillon caught hold of the wrist, turned it and the arm like a steel bar, then ran him headfirst into the railings. The man slumped to the pavement, his nose broken, blood on his mouth.

Dillon crouched beside him. "Now then, who sent you?"

"Get stuffed," the man moaned.

"You've got balls, I'll give you that." Dillon was carrying a Walther PPK in his waistband at the rear under his jacket, and now he produced it. "But I've got this, and where I come from we find a bullet through the kneecap cures most ills. A crippling experience, mind you."

"Okay." The man put a hand up. "It was Charlie Harker put us on your case. Gave us a grand to cripple you."

"Harker? And who would he be?"

"He runs everything on the river, from here down to the Isle of Dogs."

"Really?" Dillon reached inside the man's anorak, found a wad of notes and took them out. "A thousand quid from this Charlie Harker." He shook his head. "It gives me more pleasure to leave it with you than to take it."

"Screw you," the man said.

"I said you have balls. Not many brains, though. Now, if I were you, I'd call an ambulance."

He walked away, and stood on the corner thinking about it. Charlie Harker who ran everything on the river down to the Isle of Dogs? The name didn't mean a thing to Dillon. On the other hand, he knew someone to whom it very probably did. He flagged down a passing cab, told the driver to take him to Wapping High Street and got in.

He was thinking of Harry Salter, once one of the most feared men in London, a very old-fashioned gangster, now a multimillionaire from the warehouse developments he'd built on the side of the Thames. The relationship between Harry, his nephew Billy, and Dillon and Ferguson had become close, tested in the fire on a number of occasions. If anyone knew about Harker, it would be Harry Salter.

At the same moment, Charlie Harker was in a pub called the Red Lion in Kilburn in London, sitting reading the *Evening Standard* and enjoying a pint. Most people stayed well clear of him, well aware that it was best for their health. A large, heavily built man in a dark suit leaned against the wall behind him. His name was Mosby and he was Harker's minder.

Harker's mobile went. He answered it and found Ali Selim on the other end. "Mr. Harker, I must see you."

"What for?"

"The latest consignment to Iraq. I'll have to delay it for a while."

"You can't do that, it's all arranged. Leaving tomorrow night."

"It's not convenient."

"I don't care. The deal is five grand a head, so five heads makes it twenty-five, like we agreed, old son, and twenty-five is what I expect whether it's on or it's off. Does Ashimov know about this?"

"Look, be reasonable. I'll come and see you if you like. Where are you?"

"The Red Lion, but don't come without the cash. I'm beginning to worry about you, and that would never do."

Selim put the phone down and sat thinking about it. It was the thing he hated most, having to deal with people like Harker, but what could he do? It was essential to keep the traffic on the move to Iraq on a regular basis, now more than ever. At least there was the money from Ashimov to keep it going.

He found a canvas bag and opened the safe in the corner of the office. There was money in there, a great deal of money, stacked neatly in bundles of fifty-pound notes.

He counted out the required amount, put it in the bag and got his hat and a raincoat.

He was worried, running scared. He believed in what he was doing. His cause was just and he believed in Allah above everything, but all of a sudden, things seemed to have gotten out of hand. The Morgan thing had looked so promising, so absurdly simple with Ashimov's support, and not only had it failed, it had brought Ferguson and his people into the equation, and this Dillon. He shuddered. A truly frightening man. And then this business of Mrs. Morgan's so-called accident. It was a terrible business, and yet his own motives in all this had been so pure.

There was a knock on the door and the caretaker, Abdul, looked in. "Can I get you anything, Doctor?"

"No, I've got to go out for a while. I'll see you later."

He went out to the yard outside, found his Peugeot and drove away.

Dillon's cab turned from Wapping High Street and moved along a narrow lane between warehouse developments, finally stopping outside Salter's pub, the Dark Man, its painted sign showing a sinister individual in a black coat.

The bar was reasonably busy without being crowded, a fine old London pub, bright and cheerful, with Victorian gilt mirrors behind the mahogany bar, bottles ranged against them. Dora, the chief barmaid, sat on a stool behind the bar, smoking a cigarette.

"Why, Mr. Dillon. Haven't seen you for a while. They're in the corner booth."

Which they were: Harry, his nephew Billy—at twenty-nine a hard and ruthless young man, who had killed a number of times, although usually on the side of right—and Joe Baxter and Sam Hall, Salter's minders. They were playing cards, and Salter glanced up and smiled, genuine pleasure on his face.

"Why, Dillon, it's good to see you. It's been too long. You and Ferguson been up to your usual shenanigans, I assume?"

"Something like that." Dillon called to Dora. "A large Bushmills over here, love."

Billy had stopped smiling, and there was a slight frown on his face. "Trouble, Dillon?"

"How did you guess?"

"Because it follows you around and I've come to recognize the signs."

Dora arrived with the whiskey and Dillon tossed it back. "Does Charlie Harker mean anything to you, Harry?"

Salter's face turned to stone. "That scumbag. I don't mind cigarette runs or illegal immigrants from Amsterdam, but young girls on the game, porn, drugs—that's filth."

Billy said, "What is he to you?"

Dillon told them.

Afterward, Harry shook his head. "We can't have that, Charlie getting ideas above his station."

"It's not so much Harker as who put him up to it that I'm interested in," Dillon said.

Harry turned to Billy. "What do you think?"

"Friday night. That means the Red Lion in Kilburn. He uses the snug like an office. The punters turn up to pay him protection money."

"Well, let's pay him a call. It could enliven the evening."

A li Selim managed to park quite close to the Red Lion, but on the other side of the road. He was about to get out when a large Mercedes pulled up and the Salters got out. He was aware of Dillon first, and he recognized Harry and Billy Salter from photos he'd been shown. He stayed, head down, until they'd gone up the alley at the side of the pub. Only then did he get out of the Peugeot and cross to the other side. He darted into the shadows of an entrance at the end of the alley and watched as the Salters and Dillon went into the side entrance of the pub, leaving Baxter and Hall to guard the door. This was bad, very bad, he knew that and waited, his mouth dry.

I nside the Red Lion, a man was at the door of the snug, and he turned, his mouth gaping, when he saw Salter, who smiled genially.

"Why, Jacko, you look even uglier than usual." He grabbed him by the tie, swung him around, and Billy punched him very hard under the breastbone and head-butted him. Jacko went down and Billy opened the door for his uncle.

Harker was sitting at a table, counting wads of cash, Mosby leaning over beside him. They both looked up, startled.

"Why, Harry, what's going on?" Harker demanded.

"You may well ask, particularly since a couple of arse-holes claiming to be working for you just had a go at Dillon here down by Shepherd's Market, and I can't be having that because he's a friend of mine."

"I don't know what you're talking about."

"Oh, dear, so we're going to have to do it the hard way, are we?" Mosby slipped a hand inside his coat and Dillon produced the Walther. "Don't be stupid," Salter said. "Put whatever you've got in there on the table and get out, unless you'd like Dillon to leave your brains on the wall."

Mosby didn't even hesitate. He took a .38 Smith & Wesson from his pocket, laid it down and cleared off.

"Now, look," Harker said. "I don't know what's going on here, but . . ."

Salter slapped him across the face. "Bring him along, Billy, and mind the garbage on the way out."

He stood outside as Billy shoved Harker out and Baxter and Hall grabbed him. "We'll go down to my place at Wapping. I've got a nice old riverboat there, the *Lynda Jones*, but then you know that. Nice night to go on the river."

"Look, Harry, what do you want?"

"To know what you were playing at with my friend Mr. Dillon, who put you up to it."

"No way." Harker didn't sound afraid. "Leave it, Harry, you've no idea what you're getting into. The people I'm involved with could swallow you whole."

"That'd be a new sensation for me." Salter was completely unconcerned. "If I were you, I'd think about it, Charlie. Now let's go."

Standing in the doorway in the alley, Ali Selim had heard everything and it was enough. He made for the Peugeot and drove away quickly, reaching the mosque twenty minutes later. The first thing he did was call Heathrow Airport and book a first-class ticket on a plane to Kuwait that was leaving in two hours. He tossed a few things into a suitcase, together with the cash he'd taken for Harker plus his passport, and was ready to go. He hesitated, then picked up the telephone and called Ashimov, who was sitting in an Italian restaurant with Greta.

"It's me, Ali. We've got problems."

"Tell me."

Selim did. "Ferguson and his people are getting too close, and if Harker spills the beans about what he's been doing for us, it would seriously compromise Wrath of Allah."

"Don't panic. I'll handle it. Just keep cool, all right?"

Greta Novikova said, "Trouble?" Ashimov called for his bill and told her quickly.

She was worried. "Can you handle this?"

"You shouldn't need to ask. We'll take a taxi to my place, where we'll get my car and suitable weaponry. You can chauffeur me." He smiled a terrible smile. "They're only gangsters, my love. I handled them in Moscow, I'll handle them now."

Ali Selim, of course, would not have agreed with him. He rang the bell for Abdul, the caretaker, and met him on his way out to the car.

"Something's come up. I'm needed in Iraq. I'm not sure for how long, but I'll be in touch."

"As you say, Doctor." Abdul never questioned the imam's comings and goings.

Selim got into the Peugeot and drove away. The Baghdad airport, as happened so frequently, was closed to aviation traffic, which was why he was headed to Kuwait. He'd drive the rest of the way. It was surprising how cheerful he felt, the closer he got to Heathrow and away from Queen Street.

The *Lynda Jones* was moored at the other end of the wharf from the Dark Man. More than fifty years old, it had been lovingly restored, and it was the joy of Harry's life—it took him back to his childhood days as a river rat. He sat there now with Billy, at a table under an awning, and Baxter and Hall held Harker between them.

Dillon stood by the stern railing, light spilling out into the darkness, the occasional boat passing, all lit up. The whole place had a rather melancholy air to it, although, for the life of him, he couldn't think why. He shivered slightly and lit a cigarette.

Harry said, "Okay, Charlie, don't waste my time. Who told you to stick those two hoods on Dillon?"

Harker tried to struggle, and Baxter and Hall held him firmly. Billy leaned forward and slapped his face.

Harker said wildly, "I've told you, Harry, you don't know what you're getting into. This is big-time stuff, believe me."

"And who are we, the little people? Fuck this for a game of soldiers." Salter nodded to Billy. "Try the hoist and put him over."

Baxter and Hall put the struggling Harker down and Billy pulled on the stern hoist, took the hemp rope suspended from it and looped it around Harker's ankles. Baxter and Hall heaved until Harker was clear of the side, then swung him over and dropped him headfirst into the river.

He hung there for a while, struggling, weakened, then stopped. "Have him up," Harry told them.

Baxter and Hall pulled Harker out, then swung him over the rail. He lay on the deck, retching up river water.

"Had enough?" Billy demanded.

"You've signed your own death warrants," Harker said weakly.

"We're wasting our bleeding time here," Salter said. "Over with him again."

"No, for God's sake. I'll tell you."

They untied him and sat him on a chair. "Give him a fag," Salter said, which Billy did.

Dillon cut in. "So who told you to put those guys onto me?"

"A Russian called Ashimov. He runs security for that oil billionaire, Belov. Ashimov has links with Dr. Ali Selim at the Queen Street Mosque. They recruit English-born Muslims for some outfit called the Wrath of Allah. To arrange an underground route for them to Iraq or Syria. They use one of my boats to Amsterdam, then go on to Kuwait on false passports."

"You bloody bastard," Salter said. "What do you do when they come back and set bombs off in London?"

Before Harker could reply, there came a single shot. It took Harker over the rail into the water.

A shimov grabbed Greta's sleeve. "Come on, move it," and they hurried away through the shadows.

Leaving the Volvo close to the Dark Man, he and Greta had watched from the shadows and heard something of what was being said. Without hesitating, Ashimov had pulled out a Beretta, taken careful aim and fired. He seldom missed.

O n the *Lynda Jones*, the four of them crouched, waiting, and Billy reached to flick off the light switch. A moment later, they heard a car start up and move away.

"Well, that's it, whoever it was," Salter said.

"A pound to a penny it was Ashimov," Dillon said.

Billy switched on the deck lights again and they peered over. "No sign of Harker," Dillon said.

Billy shrugged. "There won't be. The tide's going out."

"Well, at least we know where we stand," Dillon said. "So if you gents will excuse me, I'll go and have words with Ali Selim. I'll keep you posted."

"No, you won't," Billy said. "I'll take you in the Range Rover."

In his quarters at the mosque, Abdul was cooking a late supper when the doorbell sounded. He went to open it and found Dillon standing there, who pushed him back and stepped in.

"Get me Selim."

"But he isn't here. He left a couple of hours ago."

"Left? Where's he gone?"

Abdul was sensible enough to be frightened. "Iraq. He said something had come up, that he was needed."

"Is that so? And when is he due back?"

"He wasn't sure. He—he said he'd be in touch."

Dillon snorted. "I wouldn't count on it."

Dillon returned to the Range Rover, and when Billy asked, "Everything okay?" told him what had happened.

"I'd say he's done a runner," Billy said. "Once you started sniffing around, that would be enough. What's next?"

"I'll call Ferguson."

When he did, Ferguson said, "The waters really are getting muddied, aren't they? I'll speak to Roper. Meet me at his place."

Dillon turned to Billy. "Regency Square."

"The Major's place? Things are starting to get interesting. Quite like old times." And he drove away.

It was shortly afterward that Abdul again answered the doorbell at the mosque and found Ashimov, who pushed past him, Greta following.

Abdul was by now extremely agitated. "He's not here. Doctor Selim has gone away."

"What in the hell do you mean, gone away?"

"To Iraq."

Ashimov was thunderstruck. "When did this happen?"

"Two hours or so ago."

"Tell me exactly what he said."

Abdul did and added, "There was someone else looking for him. A small man with very fair hair. He was very frightening."

"I bet he was," Ashimov said grimly and turned to Greta. "Let's get moving."

They got into his Volvo. "Where to now?" she said.

"Back to my place. We'll check it out. He can't be going to Baghdad, there are no commercial flights at the moment, so it has to be Kuwait."

"Then what?"

"We'll go after him. I can't go myself, Belov wants me at his place in Northern Ireland, but you can. Use our GRU contacts, they'll get you into the Baghdad airport. Use Belov's name if you need to. I'll arrange some muscle for you."

She took a deep breath. "Are you sure?"

"Smell powder again, Greta. You'll enjoy it."

"All right, I'll do it."

"Just be careful. If I were Ferguson I wouldn't let it go, this thing. He'll send somebody."

"Dillon?"

"Seems the most likely. He speaks good Arabic and Russian, has lots of Middle East experience. I'll confirm it for you."

"To hell with him. I'll still do it."

"Good girl." He was smiling as they passed Buckingham Palace. "But don't stay at the embassy. The Al Bustan is much more fun."

Ferguson, Dillon and Billy stood beside Roper's bank of computers. The Major's fingers danced over the keys for a while and he sat back.

"Definite confirmation. There was a slight delay, but the jumbo took off an hour ago. Selim has seat three-A in the first-class cabin. Nice. I can also tell you that's his fourth time to Kuwait in the last ten months."

"What else?" Ferguson demanded.

"I can give you the name of the rental-car firm he uses. It's always the same one. And he stays at the Al

Bustan hotel in Baghdad. A good hotel, though somewhat damaged by the war. A favorite with correspondents."

"Family?" Dillon added.

"Yes, there are still relatives, in a village called Ramalla about forty clicks north of Baghdad. His great-uncle lives there on a small farm by the Tigris. I've pulled a map of the location from the computer. Nicely detailed."

"Any more information on Wrath of Allah?"

"I'm still trawling. We can always try Sharif, of course."

"And who would he be?" Dillon asked.

"A major in the Republican Guard during Saddam's day. Intelligence. He's worked for me for a while now. Very expensive, but worth it. I'll give you his photo and details."

"Why not the Americans?"

"He's not keen on them. Lost his wife and daughter in the bombing during the war. He'll be of considerable value to you when you get there."

"So I'm going?"

"It's essential, dear boy, that you find Selim and haul him back," said Ferguson. "We know a great deal about him, but there's a lot more we need to know, particularly about his dealings with Ashimov and Belov."

"So you don't want me to kill him?"

"You're always so basic. No, not if it can be helped. Our Russian friends will have a different point of view, but never mind that. The Superintendent is arranging your papers now. You'll be pleased to know you're a correspondent for the *Belfast Telegraph*. You do analysis, think pieces, not instant news. Your Northern Irish accent will suit the role admirably. The Superintendent has alerted Lacey and Parry. We'll use the Citation XL. As it's RAF, it can land at Baghdad even though commercial planes are grounded."

At that moment the door buzzer sounded, and Roper pressed the release. Hannah Bernstein came in.

"Everything pushing ahead?" Ferguson asked.

"I think so, sir. They're working on Dillon's papers now, the plane will be ready for morning departure and I've spoken to Sharif. He's arranging for you to stay at the Al Bustan, which should be perfectly satisfactory."

"I don't think so," Billy said.

Ferguson frowned. "And why not?"

"Because you shouldn't be the one going. If Dillon is to pass without suspicion as a newspaper reporter, he needs a photographer with him. I mean, what he really needs is someone to watch his back, but it would be convenient, in this case, if that someone could also pass himself off as a photographer."

"And you could?"

"After Kate Rashid and company shot the hell out of me in Hazar, I had to forget my favorite hobby, diving, and so I took up photography. Did a course at the London College of Printing."

"And you think you know your stuff?"

"First of all, I'd need two cameras, if not three. I'm sure you saw the photographers during the war, draped in the damn things. As for lenses, a wide-angle zoom and a long zoom. Nikon, I think, though I wouldn't bother with digital because that would mean I'd need a laptop. Now, as far—"

"Spare me, for God's sake." Ferguson turned to Hannah. "Process his papers, Superintendent." He nodded to Dillon. "Is that all right with you?"

"Absolutely."

"Good. Since you're going in with the RAF, there won't be any problem over weapons." He said to Roper, "Have you got the Belov report ready?"

"Right here." Roper pushed five copies over.

"Excellent." Ferguson picked one up and gave it to Dillon. "Gives you something to read on the plane."

"I look forward to it."

"You take one, too, Superintendent, and you, young Salter, you'd better get home and break the good news to Harry. Now, we all have a great deal to do. I suggest we get a move on."

R AF Northolt on the edge of London catered not only to the royal family and the Prime Minister and other politicians, but was a great favorite with executive jets. So it was there the following morning that Ashimov delivered Greta Novikova to a waiting Falcon.

The two pilots were British, named Kelso and Brown, but the stewardess was Russian and introduced herself as Tania.

Ashimov kissed Greta on both cheeks. "Safe journey. I'll have someone introduce himself at the hotel. You can take it from there."

"Just one question, Yuri. Do I kill him?"

"Whatever you think best, my dear. Though it does rather seem like he's served his purpose, doesn't it?" He smiled. "Now, off you go."

Later, watching the Falcon rise, he smiled slightly to himself. What a woman. What a marvelous bloody woman. And then he turned and walked to his waiting limousine.

At Farley Field, the small RAF installation used by Ferguson's people for covert operations, Dillon, Hannah and Ferguson arrived in the Daimler and were met by Squadron Leader Lacey and Flight Lieutenant Parry standing beside a Citation XL. Both men wore flying overalls with rank tabs, and the plane had RAF roundels.

"Good to see you, Sean," Lacey said. "Will it be messy?"

"Well, you know me. It usually is."

He gave Parry his traveling bag to take on board and Lacey said, "The Quartermaster's left a bag for you inside. He said you'd find everything you need."

"Excellent," Ferguson said. "I do admire efficiency."

At that moment, an Aston Martin came around the corner of the terminal building, and Harry and Billy got out and approached, Harry carrying his nephew's bag.

"You've done it again, you little Irish sod," said Harry to Dillon. "I mean, we've had bad times before, but going to Baghdad! That's a bit rich, even for you."

He gave the bags to Parry, and Dillon said, "I'm under orders, Harry, from your man here, and Billy's a volunteer."

"Well, more fool him."

Hannah took two envelopes from her briefcase and gave them one each. "New passports, still in your real identities. They document that you've been to every war zone possible in the past few years. Your press credentials are all in order. Hopefully, Sharif will have important information for you when you arrive."

At that moment, Ferguson's mobile went and he answered it. "Yes?" He frowned. "I see. Thanks." He put it away. "Roper. A Falcon owned by Belov International took off from Northolt an hour ago with Greta Novikova on board, destination Baghdad."

"Surprise, surprise," Dillon said.

Harry embraced Billy and turned to Dillon. "Bring him back in one piece or else."

As Billy went up the steps, Hannah hesitated, then kissed Dillon on the cheek. "My God, I finally made it." He smiled. "Keep the faith."

She walked away, and Ferguson said, "Do be careful, Dillon. It would seriously inconvenience me if you didn't make it back, you and Billy both. As for Selim, if the Russians get to him, I think he's a dead man. I'm sure that's what Novikova is all about. Do what seems appropriate. Do I make myself clear?"

"You always do."

Dillon went up the steps and joined Billy. They settled down and Parry pulled up the door, then joined Lacey in the cockpit, where the squadron leader already had the engines rumbling into life.

"Here we go," Billy said. "Into the bleeding war zone again."

"Come off it, Billy, you love it."

Dillon opened his bag and produced Roper's notes. He started to read while Billy worked his way through the *Daily Mail*. It didn't take long, perhaps twenty minutes, before Dillon was finished.

"Any good?" Billy asked.

"Roper does a good job. He should write thrillers." He tossed it across. "Read it and learn what we're up against. The full and active life of Josef Belov."

IN THE BEGINNING

JOSEF BELOV

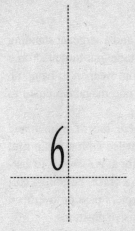

6

Once, during the early days of the Chechen War, perhaps 1991, although he could never remember exactly, Josef Belov, a colonel in the KGB and more used to intelligence work, killed five Russian soldiers personally. It happened in this way:

Belov was head of the KGB's Department 3, concerned with intelligence gathering about the Western world, but Chechnya was something else again, a case of all hands to the pumps, which was why he found himself being driven through the charnel house that was once the Chechen capital.

He sat in the front seat of an American jeep, of all things, being protected by Special Forces paratroopers, who had procured a large number of the American vehicles because of their proven worth in combat.

Belov had a corporal driving, and a sergeant standing in the back behind a heavy machine gun mounted on a swivel. He himself had an unusual weapon to hand, an Israeli Uzi machine pistol with one magazine taped to another to allow instant reloading.

There were refugees everywhere, lots of women and children, some pushing prams loaded with a few pitiful possessions, all screaming in terror at the sounds of battle: artillery shells landing with a crash, buildings collapsing in clouds of dust, helicopters passing overhead firing rockets into Chechen defensive positions.

None of this bothered Belov, the old Afghan hand. What did was the sight of a number of soldiers crowded around an army truck at the side of the road, who were obviously waiting their turn as a young girl lying back on the driver's seat was in the process of being raped.

Belov waved a hand, and the jeep stopped. He saw an older woman nearby, her face stained with blood. She struggled free of the man who held her, saw Belov and lurched toward him.

"Sir, I beg you. My daughter is only thirteen."

Two soldiers grabbed her again and pulled her back. Belov said, "Let her go."

They looked crazed, faces filthy and sweat stained. One of them cried, "Who in the hell do you think you are?" and took a pistol from his holster. Belov produced his Uzi, shot him through the head, swung as the other one pulled the woman in front of him and sprayed a short burst, which unfortunately killed the woman as

well as the soldier. The others turned in alarm and Belov
fired again and again.

Some of the soldiers started to fire back, and the sergeant returned their fire with the heavy machine gun,
scattering men across the sidewalk. The girl was still
there, Belov saw her clearly, and then the fuel tank on the
truck exploded and the whole thing fireballed. Belov's
driver immediately reversed away.

The sergeant said, "You were right to do that,
Colonel. I've got two daughters back there in Moscow."

"But I haven't. I did it because it was right in the eyes
of God. A great man named Oliver Cromwell said that
once. A general who turned England into the first republic in Europe." He took out his cigarette tin and extracted
one, passing the tin to the others. "Let's get moving.
They usually say things get better. In this case . . . I
rather doubt that."

Born in the Ukraine in 1943, Josef Belov had never
known his father, a peasant farmer who, like several
million other Soviets, had gone away to fight the war
against the Nazi invader. He never came back.

His strong extended family was held together by his
mother, and they farmed the family properties until a
number of fellow countrymen who had elected to join
the Germans turned up, and put the torch to their crops
and the buildings, killed the old men and had their way
with the women.

Belov's mother survived and made her way to Moscow, where she had relatives. What saved Belov in the years after he finished state schooling was conscription. Whatever else one could say about communism in the Soviet days, it did not waste people and their potential. It was the Red Army that discovered that Belov had a brain, nurtured him, tested him in various ways and sent him to officer cadet school, then a special department at Moscow University, where he particularly found his niche in social psychology, the science of people interacting in groups. Combined with moral philosophy, it made for an interesting mixture that, together with a flair for languages, inevitably led him into the KGB.

After 1979, when the Soviets invaded Afghanistan, he found himself heavily involved in that theater of war, and for many years he encountered an enemy, spurred on by the Taliban, who were experts in skinning alive the young conscripts who fell into their hands. Emasculation was simply a side product. At least it gave him the chance to add Arabic to his languages, but the brutality, the cruelty, the sheer barbarism, had an effect on his very soul that would not go away.

There was no time for marriage, the decencies. He was always busy—working on behalf of Department 3 in Northern Ireland, for example, feeding the Irish conflict with arms for the IRA. There were useful contacts there, especially in the Drumore area of County Louth, where the local IRA commander, a particularly hard article named Dermot Kelly, became more than useful to him over the years.

And then, in 1988, at the age of forty-five, and a major, he met Ruth.

She was twenty years younger than he and the very opposite in nature: deeply religious, as befit her biblical name, a schoolteacher and social worker concerned only with the good of others. Belov, the hard man, the soldier who had killed when necessary, adored her for her sweetness, her simplicity, her kindness.

When she had found she was pregnant, he had been over the moon, and then it had happened. She had attended a school meeting for parents one night. He'd arranged to pick her up, but then something serious had come up, KGB business, and that came first.

She'd started for home on foot in the driving rain and sleet, and somewhere on the way had been abducted, her half-naked body found in an alley close to Red Square the following morning. Standing in the mortuary looking down at her bruised and beaten face, Belov knew a horror and an anger that would never go away. It froze the soul in him, took away all humanity.

He used no police, no militia. He pulled in all the terrible power of the KGB, found the two men responsible and had them brought before him, looked on their drunken, drug-ravaged faces and knew what he must do.

They could have been charged with several offenses including her murder, could have been sent to the Lubianka, but that would have meant trials, paperwork, courts. Instead, he sent for a young lieutenant who had been allocated to him after severe wounds in Afghanistan.

Yuri Ashimov had been born in Siberia. Like Belov, conscription had been the making of him and he'd followed a similar route, which had, in the same way, taken him to Afghanistan, a terrible war, but one in which a man like Ashimov could make his mark. He couldn't believe his luck when he was allocated to Belov at Department 3, for Belov's exploits in Kabul had made him a legend.

Standing before Belov's desk, he could feel the pain, felt it as personally as if this man were a brother.

"Major, what would you like me to do?"

"I will sign an order, releasing these two animals from the Lubianka. There will be no guards, just handcuffs. Then I will wait for them at an appropriate place by the river. I will kill them personally, Yuri. What happens afterward doesn't matter to me. If I have to meet the consequences, I will."

"Well, it bothers me, Major. With due respect, I've no intention of seeing anything bad happen to one of our greatest heroes. Leave it to me, I'll get them released and your name won't be on it."

"How will you do that?"

"I have contacts, Major. And then, you said by the river? I'll bring them to the Gorsky Bridge, take the cuffs off and you can finish them."

"You would do that for me?"

"Of course, Major. It would be an honor."

And so it became a relationship that grew and flourished over the years, and when the government forces collapsed in Afghanistan in 1992, Belov, by then a colonel, and Ashimov, a captain, were among the last to leave, accompanied by another KGB colonel named Putin.

It all seemed to blur around that time, the Chechen Republic declaring independence, the carnage of the civil war, Gorbachev, the USSR ceasing to exist, the wall down in Berlin and then the mad boom years of the Russian Federation and Yeltsin, years that for the strangest of reasons were the making of Josef Belov into one of the greatest oil barons in the world and the creator of Belov International.

As the man responsible for subversive activities in the Western world, for the creation of chaos and uncertainty and fear, the events of 1991 and the first Gulf War had provided Belov with a whole new field of enterprise.

Belov had been active in Northern Ireland for some years, supplying the Provisional IRA with weaponry, linking various dissident elements with Muslim terrorist groups in the Middle East, and so on. An interesting thing about the IRA was that as the momentum of its own struggle had died down, it had left seething discontent among many of its members who, as had been the habit of the Irish over the centuries, then sought service as mercenaries overseas where their skills could be put to good use, money on the counter—and where better than the Middle East, particularly Iraq after the war. So Belov's contacts on both sides grew and flourished.

Then, after the roller-coaster years of Boris Yeltsin, everything changed. Privatization of a great deal of the Russian economy became the order of the day, and Belov didn't like it. He preferred order, discipline, a strong hand. Perhaps all the books he'd read about Oliver Cromwell had affected him more than he'd realized. So he pulled strings and moved to Baghdad, taking Ashimov with him.

It was a turbulent time, Saddam gassing the Kurds and putting down the Shiite rebellion with an iron hand. The country, of course, was suffering economically and not only from the oil embargo, and Belov could see the results. In fact, it got him interested in oil in a way he had never been before.

Sitting on the terrace at the Russian Embassy by the River Tigris having a vodka one evening, he said to Ashimov, now a major, "Yuri, have you any concept of the wealth of the oil business in western Siberia? Of the natural gas and coal and some of the richest mineral deposits in the world? Yet little of it is being developed right. Too much government interference. It's a waste, just like what's happening here in Iraq."

"I don't know about Siberia, but there's little you can do about it here, I'm afraid. If Saddam lives up to form, he's going to end up goading the Yanks and the Brits into another invasion."

"You really think he could be that insane?"

"Absolutely."

Ashimov stood up. "Now, if you'll excuse me, I have a date. Dinner and possibly dancing at Al Bustan."

"Ah, the new GRU girl, the lieutenant?"

"Greta Novikova. Quite special. Why not join us?"

The telephone on the desk rang and Belov answered, then switched into Arabic. He paused, listening, then put the phone down, frowning.

"Now, what in the hell does that mean?"

"Well, I can't comment unless you tell me."

"That was the man himself, Saddam. He wants to see me at the presidential palace."

"Which one?" Ashimov asked dryly.

Belov ignored him. "You can forget dinner. Better phone this Greta and cancel. I'll need you with me."

Ashimov was all attention now. "Of course, Colonel, at your orders," and he reached for the phone.

They drove through the city in a Range Rover, found a small crowd of people at the presidential palace and a few cars. They paused at the gates, where Belov presented his identity card and they were passed through with an efficiency that indicated they were expected. They stopped at the bottom of the huge steps leading up to the palace.

Belov said to Ashimov, "You're carrying?"

He took a Walther from the shoulder holster under his left arm and Ashimov produced a Beretta. "Of course."

Belov opened the glove compartment and put the Walther in. "And you. If we take the hardware inside, we'll set every alarm bell in the palace ringing."

They went up the steps to the entrance and found an army colonel waiting impatiently. "Colonel Belov, he keeps asking for you. This way. I'm Colonel Farouk."

The lighting was subdued, the statues in the marbled corridors only half visible in the dusk. They halted at a beaten copper doorway, a sentry on each side. The colonel went in. A moment later, he came out.

"He'll see you now, gentlemen," he said, and leaned forward and murmured in Belov's ear, "For the sake of all of us, take care, Colonel. He's in one of his manic phases. Anything is possible."

He opened the door and ushered them in. Saddam sat behind a huge desk with a shaded light as he looked up from some papers. He wasn't in uniform, and he stood up and came around the desk and spoke in Arabic, extending his hand.

"Colonel Belov, good to see you, and who is this?"

"My aide, Major Yuri Ashimov."

"Also of the KGB or the Federal Service of Counterespionage or whatever you're calling it now. Does Department Three no longer exist? I rely on Moscow."

"Excellency, you may be sure it still exists for the specific purpose for which it was created, however much our masters juggle around with changes."

Saddam's eyes glittered. It was as if he was on something, and he paced around the desk restlessly. "Sit down." He gestured to two chairs.

"It's good to know you are still operating, Belov. I have always looked on you as a friend, but these days, times are uncertain, the Americans waiting for any excuse to pounce. I've done everything they've asked for in the treaty, and what happens? The oil stays in the ground, no way of getting it out." Which was not strictly true, but he carried on. "And the exclusion zone, I'm constantly harried by their air force."

At that moment, a siren sounded in the distance and the palace was plunged into darkness. He hurried to the great windows and watched as lights turned out in patches.

"Curse them. I've never felt so impotent. And what can I do?" He turned, hands wide. "Tell me, what can I do?"

He was smiling madly, sweat on his face, turned, picked up a vacant chair and hurled it across the room in a rage and then seemed to pull himself together.

"But no, I'm a poor host. Now what about that? Women or wine? Boring. Action, passion, that's the thing. Tell me, Colonel, did you come in an embassy limousine?"

"No, Excellency, Major Ashimov drove us here in a Range Rover."

"A Range Rover?" The lights came on again, extending across the city. "It's been a long time since I drove one of those. I'm sure you'll lend it to me."

"Of course, Excellency."

"Then let's go," and Saddam led the way out.

It was a fact known only to intimates that he frequently roamed the city late at night, driving himself, often with no guards of any kind, even though Belov had heard that guards did usually attempt to follow him. Farouk was half running to keep up with him as Saddam plowed ahead.

Belov tugged on Ashimov's sleeve and they held back. "He's in one of his mad moods, so we just go with the flow. Anything can happen. We'll arm ourselves the moment we get in the Range Rover."

"As you say, Colonel."

They passed outside the main door at the top of the steps while Farouk pleaded. "Allow me to bring an escort, Excellency, that at least."

"It's a shameful thing if I can't drive through my own city without an armed guard. You will wait here."

He started down the steps to the Range Rover, and Belov paused by Farouk. "Give me your pistol." Farouk took a Browning from his holster and handed it over. "Good. Now, my advice is to follow us at a discreet distance."

In later years, he often wondered whether Saddam had seen himself as the great Caliph Haroun al Rashid in the Baghdad of old, mingling with the common people in disguise by night, but that couldn't be true, for he drove the Range Rover like a madman, scattering the crowd outside the palace, and bouncing three cars out of the way.

He laughed harshly. "I am an excellent driver, is it not so, Colonel?"

"Of course, Excellency."

Belov had the Browning in his pocket and now opened the glove compartment, passed Ashimov his Beretta and slipped the Walther into his shoulder holster.

They carved their way down into the city, swerving from one street to another, colliding with a number of vehicles, people jumping for their lives, and Saddam, in high good humor, drove even faster.

Ashimov murmured to Belov, "We're being followed."

"I know. I suggested it to Farouk."

"They're not military vehicles."

Saddam, oblivious to all this, crossed an intersection that led him onto a four-lane highway.

"Now for some real speed," Saddam cried, but at the same moment a red Ferrari accelerated beside them, a man leaning out of the rear window with a machine pistol. As he started to fire, Ashimov shot him in the head.

Another man in the front passenger seat beside the driver sprayed the Range Rover again, bursting one of the front tires. Saddam cursed, working the wheel furiously, and the Range Rover rammed into the metal road barrier and came to a halt.

A number of passing vehicles accelerated out of the way, but the Ferrari swerved, braking ahead of the Range Rover, and three men got out, all armed. At the same moment, an old white van pulled in, the rear doors opened and three more men joined the others.

Belov got out of the Range Rover and pulled Saddam with him. "Stay down, Excellency."

Ashimov joined him, his face sliced open from one

eye to the corner of his mouth. "Are you all right?" Belov asked.

"Not really." Ashimov fired twice at the ones who crouched behind the van and the Ferrari. "Traffic seems to have ground to a halt back there."

"Who can blame them."

Saddam also had blood on his face and seemed dazed. "In my own city," he said. "In Baghdad."

Belov weighed the Browning in one hand, the Walther in the other. He smiled slightly at Ashimov. "Shall we get it done?"

"Why not?"

"You take the left, I'll see to the right."

A burst of machine-pistol fire thudded into the Range Rover and he called in Arabic, "No more, Saddam is dead. I'll come out with my friend."

There was a pause, excited conversation. A voice called, "Throw out your weapons."

"We only have one gun," Belov shouted, stood up with the Walther in his left hand, and threw it toward the other vehicles, Ashimov rising beside him.

"Now," Belov said, as the six men moved into the open, and he fired very rapidly, knocking down the three on the right while Ashimov took out the three on the left. There was a movement in the van, its driver peered out and Ashimov shot him.

It was then they heard vehicles approaching fast. "Farouk and his boys," Belov said. "The cavalry arriving rather late." He took out a pocket handkerchief and gave it to Ashimov. "Best I can do."

"I'll treasure it, Colonel," and Ashimov held it to his face.

In the Ambassador's office the following morning at the Russian Embassy by the Tigris, Belov and Ashimov faced an angry man.

"You had no right to become involved," the Ambassador said. "This has gone all the way to the President in Moscow. It may not have occurred to you, Colonel, but our government's position in the Iraq situation is a very delicate one."

"I see," Belov said. "You've been informed of the circumstances. Should I have refused Saddam's invitation to the palace? I think that would have been difficult. Should I have refused to accompany him on his drive? I think not."

"Good God, man, no one appointed you to be his guardian angels. Eight men—you killed eight."

"I believe so. I would like to bring to your attention Major Ashimov's gallant conduct in this affair. As you can see, his face will never be the same again. He's lucky not to have lost an eye. I suggest he be recommended for a decoration."

"Denied," the Ambassador said. "And for the excellent reason that it never happened. That will suit Saddam, and it certainly suits our government." He paused and then carried on. "A sense of self-importance can be considered a sin in some quarters. You go too far, Colonel, and this could seriously affect your career."

The threat was implicit, but at that moment, the phone on his desk rang. He answered, listened, and the change on his face was plain.

"Of course, Excellency," he said in Arabic and put down the phone. "That was Saddam. He wishes to see you both at once."

"And do we go?" Belov asked, curiously gentle.

"I don't seem to have any choice."

"I'm sure Moscow will agree when you inform them. You will excuse us, then?" He nodded to Ashimov and led the way out.

A t the presidential palace, they were met by Farouk, who was ecstatic. "What you did was heroic, incredible, Colonel."

"You know who they were?"

"Oh, yes. Two of them were still alive and soon talked. Shiite rebels, naturally. They never stop trying. He's waiting for you eagerly."

When Farouk ushered them in, Saddam was behind his desk in full uniform. He got to his feet, came around and embraced Belov, then turned to Ashimov, examined the scar covered by gauze that ran from his eye to his mouth.

"How bad?"

"Sixteen stitches. An interesting memento, Excellency."

"I like that." Saddam laughed. "Every morning you

look in the mirror to have a shave, you'll be reminded of me. Now sit down, the both of you. I have things to say.

"I felt anger last night, but mainly impotence. I'm hedged in by the Americans and the British, even the United Nations are hardly my friends. The Shiites rebel, also the Kurds. I deal with them and people compare me to Hitler."

"Excellency, what can I say?"

"I have only one great weapon. Money. Many billions deposited in safe havens around the world, and money on that level is power."

There was a heavy pause. Belov, for want of anything better, said, "I wouldn't argue with that."

"Which brings me to the point. I owe you two my life. In my religion, this leaves me with a debt that must be repaid in some way. A sacred duty." He turned to Ashimov. "You were obeying the Colonel's instructions last night, am I right?"

"Absolutely, Excellency."

"A fine soldier doing his duty. You have my eternal gratitude. As to your future, I leave that to your colonel here—in safe hands, I think, when you hear what I have to say."

He went back behind his desk and sat, speaking directly to Belov.

"These are strange times in Russia, so many State-owned enterprises going on offer to the open market, and at such reasonable prices."

"True, Excellency."

"All my billions languish all over the world, from Geneva to Singapore, and I can't invest because of the attitude of the Americans and the United Nations. It would amuse me to outfox them."

"In what way?" Belov said carefully.

"By discharging my debt to you, Colonel, for saving my life. I understand that at the moment there are a number of oil fields up for grabs in Siberia, for sale by a government very short of the almighty dollar."

"That's true, Excellency."

"How far would one billion dollars take you?"

Belov glanced at Ashimov, who looked awestruck, took a deep breath and turned back to Saddam. "A very long way, Excellency. There could be difficulties, but difficulties are meant to be overcome. If I can serve you in any way, it would be an honor."

Saddam shook his head impatiently. "Not for me, my friend, for yourself. Don't you think my life is worth a billion dollars?"

For a moment, Belov was speechless as the enormity of it sank in, but finally managed to say, "I'm overwhelmed."

Saddam roared with laughter. "One billion? A drop in the ocean, but think what you could do. Give the damned Americans a run for their money. Now, that I would like to see. That would please me."

"But, Excellency, what can I do for you?"

"Who knows? Be my friend in bad times? A man in the shadows when needed?" There was a briefcase on the desk, and he pushed it across. "I've had my people prepare these documents in here carefully. There are code words and passwords in here that will give you access to one billion dollars."

He stood up, and Belov and Ashimov got up hurriedly. Saddam gestured at the briefcase. "Take it, Colonel." And he laughed harshly. "My debt is paid."

In the month that followed that extraordinary meeting, Belov found an excuse to visit Geneva, a certain caution in him, a refusal to believe it could be true. He took Ashimov with him, and it certainly was true, for the bankers jumped to attention.

So he returned to Moscow and resigned from the service, together with Ashimov, whom he took on as his personal aide. With all the expertise gained from so many years in intelligence, he compiled a list of the sort of people he needed to know, not only businessmen but also crooked politicians on the take, and if any such people wouldn't play ball or tried to cause trouble, there was always Yuri Ashimov of the scarred face to take care of them.

In Siberia, government contracts were readily available, especially for someone with an apparently unlimited supply of dollars. After those early deals, he never really looked back, and in the Russia of those days, no one queried them.

Within five years, the original billion had become six,

and when his old KGB friend Putin became President, it was just the icing on the cake. People didn't want democracy; they wanted strength and power and got exactly that from Putin, which suited Belov perfectly, and on his end his economic miracle suited the government perfectly, so everyone was happy.

The emergence of Al Qa'eda and the growth of the terror movement were unfortunate, for one way or another, it led to the second Gulf War and the demise of Saddam, but the prospect of the Iraqi oil fields becoming available danced enticingly in front of him, and so he was content.

The postwar turmoil in Iraq was understandable. Although the capture of Saddam by American troops seemed to herald the prospect of a more stable future, at least for Iraq, Belov had never bought the idea that the fall of Saddam would have much effect on the Arab world anyway. Muslim militants such as Al Qa'eda would still pursue what they saw as a holy war with America and the Western world, pursue that war by what they saw as the only means available to them—terror.

So Belov was pro-Arab, but only because it suited him. There was no doubt he was anti-American, but for obvious business reasons. The Brits were all right, because the Brits were the Brits and he had a weakness for London, but his old philosophy held true and was like a devil in him. To create chaos, fear and uncertainty in the Western world and in pursuit of those aims, it made sense to aid the cause of Muslim militants. But that side of things he left to Yuri Ashimov. It was not that he didn't want to know—it was just that he didn't want to know too much.

The money, of course, made all the difference. There were charitable trusts, educational trusts for young people, in reality fronts for those like Wrath of Allah, the Party of God and others, who were particularly dedicated to such enterprises as, for example, recruiting young British-born Muslims to take them to training camps in the Middle East. He had been informed of the Morgan affair in Manhattan, the intended attempt on the American President's life, an enterprise so simple it might well have succeeded if it hadn't been for the activities of Charles Ferguson and his people.

But he was separate from all that. When the Berger empire crashed, he had taken over its oil interests in southern Arabia. There was nothing America could do about that. It made him one of the most powerful businessmen in the world, highly approved of by the Russian Federation.

He had the old Rashid house in South Audley Street in London; he'd bought Drumore Place, his castle on the cliffs of Drumore in the Irish Republic, and put Dermot Kelly in charge, ostensibly as estate manager, and the money continued to roll in.

He was Josef Belov, man of mystery, unbelievably wealthy, and always at his side was Yuri Ashimov.

NORTHERN IRELAND

NANTUCKET

7

A shimov arrived at Belfast Airport in a company jet, and could have taken a helicopter onward to Drumore on the Louth coast, but instead, he'd had a car organized by his people in Belfast, or Belov's people, to be strictly accurate.

It was raining, but no surprise in that. It seemed to rain five days a week in Belfast, but he liked that and he liked Northern Ireland and the accent in which people spoke, so different from that in the Republic. It was a wonderfully beautiful place, which was why he preferred to spend a couple of hours drivng through the mountains and then crossing the border into the Irish Republic and following the coast road to Drumore.

There was a Beretta, his preferred weapon, in the glove

compartment. No border checks in these days of peace. He checked it, put it under his raincoat for easy access and drove away. The rain beat down, he turned on some music on BBC Radio, sat back and enjoyed the whole experience. There he was, born in the Ukraine, and yet he loved these crazy people.

An hour and a half later, and the Irish Sea stretched away to his left on the coast road, wind and rain driving in, and he was whistling along with the BBC when he saw Drumore Village in the distance, and the castle, Drumore Place, standing tall on the edge of the cliffs outside. It was an imposing sight, with towers and battlements and everything you would want a castle to have. There was only one problem. It wasn't particularly ancient. It had been built by Anglo-Irish Lord Drumore, wealthy from the sugar trade in the West Indies, in the early nineteenth century, his homage to the romantic tradition, and none the worse for that.

Ashimov drove down through the small port, turned into the parking lot of the local pub, the Royal George, which sounded as Orange Loyalist as you would have liked and dated from Loyalist times. But the people locally liked their traditions, and in spite of being staunchly Republican, refused to have the name altered.

As Ashimov got out of his car, a van drew up alongside. There were two young men in it. The one opening the passenger door bumped into Ashimov as he was getting out.

The youth, longhaired and unshaven and wearing an old combat jacket, got out, full of aggression.

"You want to watch it."

"I'm sorry," Ashimov said.

"Stupid prick."

Ashimov reached in the car, found the Beretta and put it in his pocket. "If you say so."

He walked to the pub entrance, and the young man and his driver burst into laughter. "I said he was a prick."

Inside, the bar was totally traditional, a beamed ceiling, dark oak booths, logs burning on the great stone hearth, an old marble-topped counter, the barman reading a newspaper, any bottle a man could fancy ranged behind him.

By one of the bow windows, a man of around fifty sat eating a meat-and-potato pie. He had red hair, a reckless look to him, and a slight smile. This was Dermot Kelly, a veteran since the age of seventeen of the Irish troubles. The man who sat in the window seat close to him, smoking and reading a book, was one Tod Murphy, who looked like some sort of intellectual, with his black hair flecked with gray, and steel spectacles. Once a student of theology intent on the priesthood, he had followed the same path as Kelly, although in his case it had included fifteen years in the Maze Prison for murdering five people. It was only the Peace Process that had released him. He looked up, saw Ashimov at the bar and smiled.

The barman, without being told, had taken a bottle of cold vodka from the bar fridge and poured a large one. Before Ashimov could touch it, the two youths who had followed him in ranged alongside him. The youth in the combat jacket picked up the glass.

"What in the hell would this be?" He drank some and made a face. "What kind of shite is that?"

"My kind, and as you've touched it, you can buy me another."

"You what?" The youth grabbed for the front of Ashimov's coat and the Russian head-butted him.

The youth went down, and his friend cried out in anger and reached for the bottle of vodka on the bar. Dermot said, "Tod."

Murphy stood up, still holding his book. "Not in here, not without Dermot Kelly's say-so. I don't know where you're from, but this is an IRA pub and this gentleman is a friend of ours."

"Fuck you," the youth said and smashed the bottle on the edge of the marble bar. Murphy kicked him under one knee and Ashimov grabbed him by the collar, screwed a short punch into his kidneys and ran him headfirst through the front door.

"Better clear the mess, Michael," Murphy said to the barman. "The terrible times we live in, Major. Kids down over the border from Belfast, always high on something. If it's not the drugs, it's the booze. But not in Drumore. We like a bit of law and order here."

"IRA law and order."

"Children can walk to school safe here, old people rest easy in their homes, young women walk home from the village dance, and with Mr. Belov the squire now, most people are in work and grateful. Farms around here are prosperous, thanks to Mr. Belov. If you were hoping to see him, he left yesterday in the helicopter for Belfast and onwards to Moscow."

"I knew."

"He's a close one, Mr. Belov."

"Because he's what you might call preoccupied with business on a worldwide scale. Anything else, he leaves to me. Now, what have you got for me?"

Tod Murphy, who as well as learning Irish in the Maze Prison had managed reasonable Russian, held up the book and said in that language, "*The City of God,* by St. Augustine. Serious reading for a serious man."

"So you still believe in God in spite of having walked over corpses all these years."

"Oh, yes," Tod Murphy said gravely. "Hell and damnation exist, redemption is possible. Christ is risen."

"As to walking over corpses, Major, we've all done that, as I understand it," Kelly told him.

"Especially Josef Belov," Ashimov said. "I think you'll find his body count exceeds the two of you put together."

"Very possibly, and I say the same of yours. But let's go up to the castle and we'll show you the ceiling they've refurbished in the Great Hall. Belov was pleased. Let's see what you think."

As they drove through the grounds, the vista was more than pleasing: the avenue of beech trees, the moat, the great entrance, the turrets, the towers. There was even a drawbridge that worked on an electronic system.

The Great Hall was everything it ought to be: a huge staircase sweeping down, carpets scattered over the flagged floor, two enormous chandeliers hanging from the gilded ceiling, a log fire smoldering on the wide hearth, an oak table, twelve chairs around it, a couch on each side of the fire.

"You'll have a drink?" Kelly asked. "The kitchen's working on the lunch now."

"Why not?"

"And you can tell us why you've come," Murphy said.

"What do you know about a man named Sean Dillon?" Ashimov asked.

Tod Murphy simply stopped smiling and looked astonished. "Sean? What in the hell is he to you?"

Dermot Kelly laughed out loud, and Ashimov said, "What is this? It sounds as if he's some kind of friend."

"Ah, Major, you'll never understand the Irish. Sean was more than a friend. He was the best, a true comrade," Kelly said. "We were on the run from Brit paratroopers in the sewers of Derry on one famous occasion. I took a bullet in the shoulder, but I could keep going. Tod here got one in the leg and fell by the wayside. When Sean found out, he went back for him."

"I'll drink to him any day," Murphy said.

Ashimov was bewildered. "This man works for Charles Ferguson, who heads the Prime Minister's secret security service. So secret, it's known in the trade—"

Kelly cut in, "—as the Prime Minister's private army, and they'd need the best, so they got Sean."

"I don't understand you."

"You'd need to be Irish to understand us, Major, and it's got nothing to do with religion. Sean Dillon is the best. They couldn't touch his collar for years, not the RUC, not the British Army. D'you know how he ended up working for Ferguson? During the Serb War, he was flying medical supplies in for children, the Serbs caught him."

"It's what's called a good deed in a naughty world," Tod Murphy said. "He was faced with a firing squad— and Ferguson blackmailed him. He saved his skin, wiped his slate clean, and in return Sean became his enforcer. We all know the story."

And Ashimov, in spite of his wealth of experience, was astonished. "And you don't mind?"

Kelly said, "I told you. He was a comrade. The best. But if he got you in his sights, you were dead. Still would be."

"So why do you want to know about him?" Kelly asked, and Ashimov told them.

When he had finished, Murphy said, "So this Ali Selim bowser is on the run in Iraq and you've got what's-her-name, Greta Novikova, on his tail?"

"Ferguson will have Sean on that one like a dose of salts," Kelly put in. He turned to Tod Murphy. "Put your priest's intellect on this. What's your conclusion?"

"Quite simple. Ferguson doesn't want a trial at the Old Bailey. The Muslims wouldn't like that. He's sent Sean to bring Selim back. A nice, quiet inquisition in some safe house in London, and you and Mr. Belov wouldn't like that."

"Well, let's hope it doesn't come to that. But how would you two feel if I had trouble in London with Ferguson and his people? What would you say if I said I needed you? It would include taking on Dillon."

They looked at each other and smiled.

"Ah, now," said Murphy. "He was a comrade, to be sure. But that doesn't mean there might not be a score or two to settle."

"Things run well here, as you know," Kelly said. "We do things our way and Belov's money for the farmers keeps things sweet."

Tod cut in. "But with the Peace Process, it gets awfully boring. What you suggest could be interesting."

"But just so you realize," Kelly added. "If there's something Sean Dillon could give master classes in, it's bloody mayhem."

"So where would that leave you?"

"Oh, we'd give him a run for his money." And Tod Murphy smiled.

It was later that day that President Jake Cazalet walked on the shore at Nantucket. He loved the old beach house with its seafront of beach and sand dunes, and came down whenever he could, certainly most weekends. The helicopter delivered him from Washington late on a Friday, picked him up again Sunday evening.

He had a cook and housekeeper in from the local town. No fuss and good plain cooking, he would say. He'd always insisted that only two Secret Service men accompany him and one always had to be Clancy Smith. The other usually handled communications.

Even with only two minders, however, the security around him was electronically state-of-the-art, especially since the assassination attempt on him three years before while running through the nearby marsh.

He was walking on the beach now with his beloved flat-coated retriever, Murchison, and with Clancy Smith. The surf boiled, the sky was slate gray, rain showering in so hard that the two men each carried an umbrella. They paused for Clancy to light the President's cigarette.

"It feels good to get away from everything, Mr. President."

"My God, but it does. The smell of that salt in the air is really something."

"It sure is."

In the distance came the unmistakable sound of a helicopter approaching. Clancy said, "That will be Blake coming in, sir."

"And our English cousins," Cazalet said. "It always gives me a strange feeling when I hear those things." He looked along to where the helicopter was dropping in on the beach. "Takes me right back to Vietnam." He flicked his cigarette away. "Okay, let's go and greet our guests."

Ferguson and Hannah Bernstein sat together on the other side of the coffee table by the fire, Cazalet facing them, Clancy leaning against the wall by the French windows behind. Murchison lay on the rug, watching.

Cazalet said, "I read Major Roper's report on Josef

Belov with interest, if that's the right word. I've spoken to the Prime Minister only briefly, for obvious reasons."

"Which is why he thought it a good idea that we talk, Mr. President."

"Thank God we do, otherwise I could have been dead on that sidewalk in Manhattan. It could have succeeded so easily. I'll never understand it, the drive to assassinate."

"Actually, the Superintendent knows a bit about it," said Ferguson. "She has a master's degree in psychology."

Cazalet said, "Superintendent?"

"Motive, sir, is the basic requirement."

"And hate," Cazalet said. "Deep conviction."

"Not always," she replied. "For one kind of assassin, professional, the motive is usually money, and a target like you would be a big payday. But the money is no good if he doesn't survive. It's often a *Day of the Jackal* kind of thing for them—meticulous planning and a guaranteed exit."

Cazalet nodded. "And the other kind?"

"Usually the most successful. You'll remember President Reagan, shot at close quarters by a man in the crowd who knew he would stand no chance of getting away."

"So we're back with what I said in the first place. The motive is hate, deep conviction."

"And often a genuine religious belief. It's interesting that the word *assassin* is derived from the Arabic. During the Middle Ages, members of various cults under the influence of hashish attempted to kill many leaders of the Crusades."

"Jewish zealots in biblical times used the same tactics on the Romans," Ferguson put in.

Hannah said, "It can derive from a feeling of deep frustration, Mr. President. It was Lenin who said the purpose of terrorism is to terrorize. It's the only way a small country can fight against an empire."

"That was one of Michael Collins's favorite sayings when he led the IRA back in 1920 against the British," Ferguson said.

Cazalet nodded. "All very interesting, but how does it explain Morgan?"

"I don't know any religion on earth that doesn't have its extremists," Hannah said. "Right through history, and usually those extremists are the kind of people who are extremely good at brainwashing others, particularly young people."

"Into becoming assassins, suicide bombers?" Cazalet shook his head.

"Of course, the religious leaders who spread the word are usually reluctant to put themselves on the line."

"Understandably." Cazalet got up. "I arranged a light lunch with cook and gave her the afternoon off. I wanted us to have privacy. It's waiting for us in the kitchen. Lead the way, Clancy. You'll join us, of course."

The conversation over lunch was much more social and pleasant, ranging from what was worth seeing on the West End stage to Cazalet and Hannah comparing student days at Harvard and Cambridge.

Cazalet turned to Ferguson. "Did you go to university, General?"

"Too busy. I always intended to, but we had conscription then. After two years in the army, I got a taste for it, I suppose. I was eighteen and Communist Arabs were shooting at me, so when they offered me a commission . . ." He shrugged. "It seemed the natural thing to do."

"All those rotten little wars," Hannah couldn't help saying. "You couldn't get enough."

"Ah, there speaks the psychologist," Ferguson said cheerfully. "But not *my* rotten little wars, my dear. All the way through, and that includes Northern Ireland, Bosnia, Kosovo and the two Gulf Wars, I was a member of that happy band of brothers called soldiers who take care of those things from which the general public turns its face. I've always liked to think it an honorable profession." He smiled at Cazalet and Clancy. "Of course, I do not include the marines in that sentiment."

"We thank the General," Clancy said, and they all laughed, but Hannah was uncomfortable and it showed. The trouble was that she was changing inside herself and her head and she didn't know what to do about it.

Cazalet, sensing something wasn't right, smiled at her reassuringly and stood up. "Okay, folks, to work," and he led them back to the sitting room.

So, if I'm getting this right," he said a while later, "this Dr. Ali Selim, sensing personal disaster, has fled to Iraq. We're aware that he has been controlled by this Major Yuri Ashimov, who is head of security for the Belov organization. Which I assume means a plentiful source of financial support for Muslim extremist groups."

"There's no possibility of proving that in a court of law, Mr. President," Hannah said.

"It's just about impossible to touch Josef Belov," Ferguson said. "He's far too powerful, one of the richest men in the world, and a friend of Putin."

"Even if it was revealed that he'd donated money to some of these Muslim organizations," Hannah said, "it would be impossible to prove that he'd acted except in good faith."

"So where does that leave us?" Cazalet asked.

"The most worrying aspect is the recruitment of young British Muslims to join militant groups in the Middle East," Ferguson said. "To be trained in camps in Syria or Iraq, even in southern Arabia, and then returned to Britain and America, often as sleepers, to lead apparently normal lives until their special abilities are required. Cannon fodder for Al Qa'eda."

"You think Wrath of Allah is part of that?"

"It wouldn't surprise me. We know a great deal about them and a great deal about Belov, as you've read. Don't forget that when he was with the KGB, he was totally dedicated to helping the downfall of all Western values. A kind of old-fashioned Bolshevik. He's got all the money in the world, so money is only a means to an end."

"But what's the point?" Cazalet demanded. "Why behave as he does?"

"The game, Mr. President," Hannah said. "The game

is the thing. The ultimate power of being able to move his way around the chessboard and laugh at us all, be untouchable."

"So what do we do about it?" Cazalet asked.

Ferguson said, "Sending that GRU major, Novikova, on Selim's trail to Baghdad probably means the worst. That Selim's served his purpose and knows too much. I imagine they'll finish him off if they can, though I'm not completely sure of that."

"Which is why you've sent Dillon. To save him?"

"Dillon will do what seems appropriate in the circumstances. If that means saving him, fine, and if that means making sure Selim meets a bad end, so be it. If Selim can be retrieved, there's always the possibility of squeezing more information out of him about the Belov connection." He shrugged. "If not, he's dispensable."

Cazalet said, "Whichever way it goes, it's going to get very nasty."

"Exactly, Mr. President, but that's what my organization was set up for all those years ago. We're responsible only to the Prime Minister. Nobody else can touch us—the Security Services, the Ministry of Defence, even Parliament."

"A license to kill," Cazalet said.

"If that's what it takes. We're dealing with global terrorism. It's a whole new threat, and we can't cope with it by playing according to the rule book."

"I totally agree, Mr. President," Blake said.

"The Prime Minister's made it plain that I'm in

charge and that I'm to take any steps that seem appropriate. That, in effect, is why I'm here. He wanted to make it clear to you that such an attitude will reflect our policy in the future."

"So you'll forget the legal system, the courts and everything that goes with it?"

"Desperate times call for desperate remedies."

Cazalet turned to Hannah. "From what I've come to know about you, Superintendent, I'd say such an attitude might give you a moral problem."

"It does, sir. In a troubled world, it seems to me that if we don't have the law, a justice system, we have nothing."

"Which is exactly what our enemies count on," Ferguson replied. "It's a question of survival. We either fight back or go under. Anyway, that will be our plan of action from now on. The Prime Minister wanted you to know."

Cazalet turned to Blake. "You agree with all this?"

"I'm afraid so, sir. Everything we stand for, all our values, are on the line these days. As the General says, we fight back, or go under."

"I thought you'd say that." Cazalet sighed. "Okay, General, anything we can do."

"We're together on this, Mr. President?"

"We always have been."

"And Belov?" Blake put in. "He's pretty untouchable."

"Nobody is untouchable." Cazalet wasn't smiling now. "Take him down, gentlemen, whatever it takes."

Three hours later, rising up from Andrews Air Force Base in the Citation and leveling at fifty thousand feet, Ferguson unfastened his seat belt and smiled at the pretty young RAF sergeant standing over him.

"I'll have a large Scotch, my dear." He turned to Hannah on the other side of the aisle. "What about you, Superintendent?"

"I don't think so, sir. I'm having difficulty enough keeping my head straight."

"Right now, Superintendent, even as we speak, Dillon and young Billy Salter are out there in harm's way dealing with some very nasty people."

"I know that, sir."

"Then you'll have to decide which side you're on. It's up to you, Superintendent." And he drank his whiskey.

IRAQ

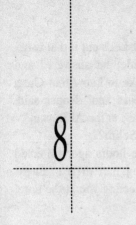

8

An hour out of Baghdad, the Citation down to thirty thousand feet, Billy was reading Roper's report for the fourth time. Dillon had found a half bottle of Irish whiskey in the bar box and poured a large one.

Billy closed the report. "This guy Belov, his bleeding life's been a saga, and Ashimov—he'd kill the Pope, wouldn't he?"

"I'd agree with you. I'd say he was the one who pushed Mrs. Morgan off that jetty."

"And this Novikova woman?"

"A looker, Billy, but don't be fooled. You don't make major in the GRU by being soft. That's why Ashimov's rushed her to Baghdad."

"To take care of Selim."

"He's a walking dead man."

"And where's that leave us?"

"They'll be expecting us, Billy. Let's put it that way."

The telephone rang at his side; he answered and found Roper. "I thought you'd like to know that Greta Novikova landed safely four hours ago," Roper said. "She didn't go to the embassy. She's at the Al Bustan."

"Well, that's nice. What about Selim?"

"Dropped in at Kuwait twelve hours ago, collected his car and set off north. It's a long, hard drive to Baghdad these days, Sean. Sharif is meeting you at the hotel early evening."

"Thanks."

"Have fun."

Dillon replaced the phone. Billy said, "What was that?"

Dillon told him.

Billy was highly amused. "What are we going to do about Novikova? Have a drink in the bar?"

"Who knows? Stranger things have happened."

"Another thing, those two IRA geezers at this Drumore Castle. Did you know them in the old days?"

"You could say that."

"Friends or enemies? I mean, if Ashimov asked them to try and blow your head off, would they do it?"

"Yes."

"For a price?"

"That and the game, Billy." Dillon poured another whiskey. "Especially if they couldn't think of anything better to do."

"Crazy," Billy said. "All you Micks are crazy."

Parry appeared. "Landing in fifteen minutes. It'll be a very fast descent, so strap up well." He smiled. "It's the missiles, the ones some peasant fires from his shoulder. We'd just as soon avoid them if we could."

"That really makes my day," Billy said. "Thanks very much," and did as he was told.

But the landing went perfectly. Baghdad looked like most large airports except for the guards, the gun pits, the hardware heavily on display everywhere and lots of military aircraft. They taxied to the main RAF area, parked under instructions and Lacey switched off.

Parry left the cockpit and opened the door. "Good flight, huge tailwind. We're over an hour early." An RAF Land Rover drove up to meet them and a sergeant got out in camouflage battle dress and saluted Lacey.

"If you gentlemen will get in, I'll see to the luggage and take you to the mess. Parker's my name."

"What about transport down to town?" Dillon asked.

"Taken care of, sir, what we call a safe taxi. You'll be fine. It's been quiet lately."

They were drinking very English tea in the RAF mess, eating biscuits with Lacey and Parry, when a flight lieutenant turned up.

"I'm Robson—police." He shook hands with Lacey. "Haven't seen you since Kosovo. Heard about your Air Force Cross. Good show." He turned to Parry. "We've never met, but good show, too. I've seen your priority rating—higher even than the Prime Minister turning up. I've been in the RAF long enough to know it doesn't pay to ask questions. You chaps are obviously moving in very exalted circumstances. Mr. Dillon?"

"That's me."

Robson handed him an envelope. "A red Security One tag. It covers everything."

"Everything?"

"Oh yes, immediate response if you're in trouble, and I presume you gentlemen could be?" He handed a similar envelope to Billy. "Mr. Salter."

"I feel a whole lot better," Billy said.

Robson turned back to Dillon. "There's a safe taxi parked outside with Sergeant Parker at the wheel in civvies. He'll be on line. Mobile number in your envelopes. Twenty-four-hour watch." He turned to Lacey and Parry. "I've had special instructions. Informed General Ferguson at the MOD that you'd landed and was told you two were to stay and wait here, the Citation refueled for instant takeoff when required."

"So they can't go to downtown Baghdad and have a drink with us?" Dillon asked.

"Too dangerous, old boy," Robson said.

"Of course," Billy told him. "This just gets better all the time."

"Your bags are in the taxi, gentlemen, no inspection at the gate." He smiled. "But why would there be? You're just a journalist and a photographer." He got up. "All I can say is enjoy."

The run to Baghdad itself was calm enough, with plenty of traffic, a lot of it local—cars, trucks and vans, plus lots of donkeys loaded with produce, peasants walking beside them. It was late afternoon, but they were headed for tomorrow's markets in Baghdad. Rounding it all off were military vehicles of every kind everywhere.

Dillon said to Parker, "So tell us the worst, Sergeant."

"Well, I'm an old hand. Served in both Gulf Wars, Bosnia and Kosovo in between. If you think things are better because the Yanks grabbed Saddam, you'd be wrong. Plenty of Iraqis were pleased about that, but lots weren't and they still hate each other. Sunni Muslims, Shiites, stir in a few Kurds, mix it with so-called 'Muslim freedom fighters' from all over the world, and that's not even counting Al Qa'eda."

"You shouldn't have joined," Billy said.

"Well, I did." Parker laughed. "And you know what? I love every bloody awful minute of it." He hesitated. "I'm not supposed to ask, but, well, I spent fifteen years in the RAF police. I've been around the houses."

"Which means?" Dillon said.

"Well, you *sound* Northern Ireland. I should know, because I did four tours there. But *Belfast Telegraph*? I doubt it. As for Mr. Salter, with the greatest respect, he's been around the block as well."

"I'm surprised you haven't made warrant officer," Dillon said.

"I once had a falling-out with a warrant officer and punched him." Robson opened the glove compartment in the car and produced a Browning. "Should I keep this handy?"

"Very sensible."

"Thank God. Things have been getting boring lately."

Baghdad was Baghdad. The streets all seemed to be some kind of a market, the traders' voices high as they shouted to passersby, music blaring out from scores of shops, and traffic everywhere, so much of it that they were reduced to a crawl.

"Is the Al Bustan far?" Dillon asked.

"Which one? There are several. It's a very common name. Still, don't worry, I know the right one."

The evening dusk was setting in as they finally moved off a road not far from Al Rashid Street in the old quarter and turned up a narrow lane and halted at a gate that stood open but had a bar across it. An Iraqi peered out of a small hut and took his time coming.

"Get it up, for Christ's sake," Parker told him.

The man said something pretty basic in Arabic, and Dillon reached out through the open window, grabbed him by the throat and told him exactly what to do in reasonably fluent street Arabic himself. The startled man staggered back, got the bar up and Parker drove on.

The hotel was very old-fashioned, the grounds quite large, with a swimming pool and a number of cottage apartments dotted around surrounded by palm trees.

They coasted up to the main entrance, braked to a halt, and a couple of porters came down the steps to meet them and take the luggage. Parker didn't get out.

He said to Dillon. "*Belfast Telegraph*? I never heard Arabic like that on the Shankill."

"We spoke it on the Falls Road all the time."

"I'm sure you did." Parker smiled. "I look forward to hearing from you," and drove away.

The reception area was very old-fashioned as well, with three great fans hanging from the ceiling and swirling around. In the taxi, Billy had extracted two cameras from his bag and had slung them around his neck. He took a couple of pictures of the foyer and moved to an archway opening into a huge bar and café area. He took more pictures and turned to Dillon.

"Brilliant. Just like *Casablanca*. All we need is Rick."

"You've made your point, Billy."

The man behind reception interrupted. "Gentlemen, my name is Hamid. I am the manager. May I help you?"

"Dillon and Salter," Dillon told him.

"Ah, Mr. Dillon. We weren't expecting you yet."

"Hell of a tailwind," Billy put in.

Dillon lit a cigarette. "Is there a problem?"

"Not at all. Cottage Five."

"I was hoping to meet Miss Novikova." Dillon said it in Arabic, and Hamid was startled. "She's arrived, I know that."

"Yes, she arrived a few hours ago. Cottage Seven." He

snapped his fingers to the two porters, who picked up the bags and led the way out, Billy and Dillon following, down a narrow path leading through the palm trees. They saw tables beside the pool, sheltered by umbrellas, people sitting around having drinks. As the porters forged ahead, Dillon pulled Billy close to him.

"The end table with the green-and-white umbrella. The woman in a light blue dress sitting with what looks like an Iraqi. Black hair, bushy mustache."

"Yes?"

"That's Greta Novikova."

"And the guy?"

"Sharif. I've seen his photo. Keep moving."

They passed on, following the porters to the cottage. One of the porters unlocked the door and they led the way in. It was all very acceptable. A sitting room, two bedrooms and a shower room. There was even a small kitchen and a terrace.

Dillon paid the porters off, unlocked the French windows and moved out onto the terrace. Billy joined him. "What do you think about Novikova?"

"I don't know, Billy, except that she shouldn't be so cozy with Sharif."

"So what do we do?"

"Unpack, have a shower—you can go second—and speak to Sharif when he turns up. After that, venture out into the bar, and who knows? We might just bump into Novikova."

Billy smiled. "Harry's right, you are a sod."

Toward the end of her flight, Greta had received a call from Ashimov. "Ah, the wonders of cyberspace. It's just as I thought. Dillon's on his way to Baghdad, too. I've even got his estimated time of arrival."

"I'm impressed."

"To the great Ashimov, anything is possible. I've arranged for two mercenary friends of mine in Baghdad, Igor Zorin and Boris Makeev, to handle the dirty work."

"Are they good?"

"Ex-paratroopers, good Chechen experience. They'll do. Like you, Dillon is staying at the Al Bustan. He's got a backup with him, that young gangster, Billy Salter. They're posing as press."

"Isn't that going to be awkward, them staying here, too?"

"Not really. He'd have run you down soon enough. The beauty of it is that the manager at the Al Bustan, a guy called Hamid, has worked for me many times before. He's already informed me that a Major Sharif, a former Republican Guard, was making inquiries about Dillon's arrival. I gave Hamid instructions to speak to this man on my behalf. To seduce him with money. You like it?"

"Poor Dillon."

"You'll have plenty of time to speak to Sharif before Dillon and Salter get there. Stay in touch."

At the Al Bustan, Hamid couldn't do enough for her, the magic name of Belov pervading the air. He took her to her cottage personally, then called Major Sharif on his mobile. Greta didn't bother to unpack; instead she simply went and sat at the table by the pool and ordered a large vodka cocktail from a passing waiter. She was sipping it, thinking, when Sharif approached and introduced himself. He was a large man in his forties, with black hair and mustache, and sad eyes. He wore a creased linen suit, and the bulge in the right-hand pocket indicated a weapon.

He half bowed. "Major Novikova?"

"Major Sharif. Please sit. Would you like a drink?"

When he had sat, she said, "I don't like to waste time, so listen carefully." She filled him in with a few terse sentences. "Do you know Zorin and Makeev?"

"I've seen them around. They're the kind who turn their hand to anything."

"What about Selim in Ramalla?"

"I've already made inquiries. I have contacts in the area. His great-uncle is expecting him tonight."

"Tell Dillon he's arriving tomorrow. We'll meet here later with Makeev and Zorin and decide on our next move. And let's be clear: Ferguson may pay you well, but if you want top dollar, Josef Belov pays more." She smiled. "In case you were wondering."

"I am very content, Major." He took out a card. "My mobile number. Give me yours." She did.

"Good. Call me as soon as you hear he's arrived."

"Of course."

He half bowed and walked away.

Showered and changed into a fresh shirt and a tan linen suit, Dillon went through the hardware bag from the quartermaster at Farley Field, found a Walther, checked it out and slipped it into his right jacket pocket. He went out on the terrace, lit a cigarette and Billy joined him.

"I'm hungry. When do we eat?"

At that moment, Sharif came along the path through the palm trees.

"Mr. Dillon?"

"That's right."

"I'm Major Sharif. You arrived early. Sorry I wasn't here."

Dillon put a hand on Billy's shoulder. "That's okay, no big deal, was it, Billy?"

Billy responded well. "Hell, no." He held out his hand. "Good to meet you."

Dillon said, "There's one thing straightaway. I've heard from London that Greta Novikova is staying here."

"I've only just heard that myself. I've just checked in for the night and the manager told me. We have an arrangement. He does me favors."

"But you wouldn't know her?"

"No. I don't think she's worked in Baghdad before."

"I see. So, what about Selim? Is he turning up here?"

"He would have booked ahead, and he hasn't. I expect

he's still driving up from Kuwait, and I think he'll go straight to his uncle's place in Ramalla. He'll probably arrive tomorrow, but I'll have better information later."

Dillon smiled and patted him on the shoulder. "No, me ould son," and he nodded to Billy, who took out a Walther and stood with his back to the door. "I think you've got better information now."

Sharif knew a real pro when he saw one and sighed heavily, not even angry. There was a kind of resignation to him.

"Could I have a drink, Mr. Dillon? I'm that kind of Muslim."

Dillon found a bottle of Scotch in the bar box and two glasses and poured. Sharif drank it down. He held the glass out and Dillon poured another.

Sharif said, "I was a Republican Guard and military intelligence under Saddam, because we all have to get by in life, which means I was a bad boy. But then I lost my wife and my daughter in the bombing, and that was the war, so fuck Saddam and fuck all of you, the Americans, the Brits and now the Russians, for ruining my country."

"I appreciate the point." Dillon toasted him. "As it happens, I'm Irish—IRA Irish, so I can be your worst nightmare. With the credentials I've got, I could turn you in to the Yanks, and I'm sure they'd like to have you."

"And the alternative?"

"Work with us and I'll guarantee that Ferguson will pay you as agreed and give you a clean slate. Mind you, he'll expect you to continue working for him."

Sharif was astounded. "Can this be true?"

He turned to Billy, who shrugged. "Don't look at me. I just kill people when he tells me to."

"The world's gone crazy."

"So they tell me," Dillon said. "Are you in or out?"

"I'm in."

"Good man. Now tell me what happened between you and her."

Sharif did, and Billy said, "Zorin and Makeev sound like trouble."

"That's why I have you, Billy." Dillon went to the quartermaster's hardware bag, took out a file, opened it and selected a computer printout. "Does this look familiar?"

Sharif looked surprised. "Why, that's Ramalla, and that's the Selim farm just outside in the orange grove by the river. It was damaged in the war, but the old man still lives there on his own. Women relatives call in to see to his needs, so my contact informs me."

Dillon went back to the bag and opened a false bottom that contained ten thousand American dollars operating money. He took out two thousand in fifties and handed it over.

"That's to be going on with."

Sharif looked astonished, but stashed the money away. "What can I say?"

"How long to Ramalla?"

"It's forty kilometers, an hour, could be less. You want me to take you?"

"No, I have a driver who knows his way around. What I want you to do is check with your contact and call me on my mobile the moment you hear Selim's arrived. We'll be ready and waiting to go."

"And Novikova?"

"Call her half an hour later. Billy and I will be a nice surprise for her and her friends when they turn up."

"Couldn't we just grab Selim and scarper?" Billy demanded.

"Not if we want to rub Ashimov's nose in it. He'll have a lot of explaining to do to Belov." He turned to Sharif. "Off you go, then."

Sharif said, once again slightly bewildered, "You trust me, Mr. Dillon?"

"Let's say you strike me as an honorable man. But don't forget to tell her you've told me there's no chance of Selim before tomorrow. In the meantime, Billy and I will sample the delights of the Al Bustan restaurant and bar. It's been a long day."

Sharif went out, shaking his head, and Dillon called Sergeant Parker on his mobile.

"It's Dillon. Do you know a place called Ramalla?"

"I certainly do."

"You're taking us there tonight. Dress in civilian clothes and don't forget the Browning."

"Like that, is it? If I leave now, I could be with you in an hour."

"Dress smartly, old son. Remember it's the Al Bustan."

"You've got to be joking." Parker laughed and switched off.

Dillon then tried Lacey and tracked him down in the mess. "Dillon here. How's everything with you?"

"There are some interesting people around, but otherwise it's boring. Since we're on standby, we can't have a drink. Whatever you're up to, do get on with it, old lad."

"I can't promise, but somewhere around midnight could be a possibility. Would that give you a problem?"

"Red Priority One? Sean, they all jump to that."

"There's a possible passenger, but that would imply perfection in an imperfect world."

"We're entirely in your hands. Take care."

Dillon snapped his Codex Four shut and turned to Billy. "That's it for now. Let's try that bar."

9

Sharif, the old intelligence hand, decided to brave Greta Novikova face-to-face, and knocked on the door of Cottage Seven. She opened it, dressed in a bathrobe, a towel around her head.

"I've seen them," he said.

"You'd better come in and tell me everything."

Which he did, or his version of everything. "He's a hard one, this Dillon."

"More than you'll ever know. But the important thing is you've made it clear that Selim won't be there until tomorrow."

"Absolutely. He'd no reason not to believe me."

"And any news from Ramalla?"

"As I said, definitely later tonight. I'm going to check

my sources now. I have police contacts in the area. A matter of some delicacy."

"Then get on with it. I have Zorin and Makeev turning up soon." She opened the door for him. "What is Dillon doing now?"

"He told me they were going to the bar."

"I'm sure he would."

She let him out, stood there frowning for a moment, then went into the bedroom and started to dress.

The bar and restaurant area was hardly busy, with no more than a couple of dozen people scattered around the tables, three or four on bar stools. The fans stirred on the flaking ceiling, the ornate mirrors at the back of the bar were cracked in places, and here and there the wall was pockmarked with bullet holes, but the two barmen wore white jackets, the headwaiter a tuxedo. They were all trying. The war, after all, was over.

Billy had two cameras slung around his neck and snapped away with genuine enthusiasm, going out through the open French windows to the terrace and the floodlit pool area. He returned.

"Great, Dillon, just great. We could make a movie."

Dillon had discovered an acceptable bar champagne and toasted him. "Just your thing, Billy. You'd look great in a white tuxedo. We'll get Harry to put up the money."

And then Greta Novikova walked into the bar, elegant in a very simple black silk dress that was short, but not too short, set off by gold high-heel shoes, with her hair tied back.

"I was wondering where you'd got to," Dillon said. "But it was worth the wait, girl. You look grand."

"You're a cheeky bastard, Dillon, I'll say that for you. I'll have champagne on the terrace."

She walked out, heads turning, and selected a table and Dillon ordered a bottle of Dom Perignon from the headwaiter.

"Ferguson is obviously extremely generous when he allows you to order stuff like that," Greta said.

Billy was seated on the balustrade, snapping away. "Oh, Dillon's the man for you. He's got plenty stacked away."

As the headwaiter uncorked the bottle and a waiter brought three glasses, Dillon said, "That's a great lie, or part of a one. Billy here and his uncle Harry have millions in property development by the Thames, but he's a boy of simple tastes. Prefers being a photographer."

"Photographer, my ass," she said to Dillon in Russian.

"And what was that all about?" Billy asked.

"I couldn't bear to tell you," Dillon said. "But it was rude." He turned to the headwaiter. "Only two glasses. The boy doesn't drink."

"No, he just shoots people when the mood takes him," Greta said, and sipped some of her champagne. "I know very well who you are. Your uncle is one of the most notorious gangsters in London, and you're not far behind."

"I'll have to run faster, then."

Dillon produced a pack of Marlboros and gave her a light. "So where do we go from here? You know what the game is, or think you do."

"But my game could be different from yours. We Russians can be very devious." She emptied her glass in a quick swallow. "Not vodka. Now, there's a real drink. Buy a bottle and I'll trade glass for glass with you."

Billy was laughing. "You're one of a kind, lady. Go on, Dillon, give it a go."

And Dillon liked her, liked her more than any woman in a long time, as she leaned across the table so close that he could smell her perfume, her chin on one hand. "Come on, Dillon." She was challenging him now. "Would you like to give it a go?"

There was a pause, then Dillon said, "I capitulate." He ordered a bottle of vodka, which was provided almost instantly.

She insisted on having the first one. "I am the taster." She took it straight back, Russian style, and made a face. "Now, this one they've made in some backyard in Baghdad. Try it, Dillon."

He did, and it burned like fire. He coughed, tears in his eyes. "Well, it's not Irish whiskey, but it'll do to take along. Let's save some for your friends. They'll be joining you, I'm sure." She poured him another with a steady hand. "Makeev and Zorin."

"Sounds like a variety act," Billy said.

"Ah, Mr. Salter, there you would be making a mistake. They come highly recommended."

Two men came out through the French windows,

strangely similar in black shirts and tan suits, around forty, hard and fit with military-style haircuts.

The nearest one said in Russian, "Major Novikova. Igor Zorin. This is Boris Makeev."

"Make it English. Mr. Dillon here speaks Russian almost as well as you do."

"A man of taste, which doesn't extend to his choice of vodkas," Makeev said. "But when you're Irish, anything's better than nothing, I suppose."

Makeev drank from the bottle, made a face and spat it out onto the table, spotting Greta's dress. "Control yourself," she said angrily. "That's an order."

"We're not in the army now," Makeev told her. "We're working for wages, and I can tell you we don't take kindly to women who try to give orders."

Billy took a step toward him, and Dillon said, "Leave it."

Sergeant Parker appeared through the French windows, wearing a dark blue blazer and flannel slacks. He put his right hand inside the blazer and stood, silent and watchful.

"Nothing to say?" Makeev asked.

"Your hair fascinates me," Dillon said. "Shaved off like that, the two of you look like a couple of convicts on the run. Now, the SAS at Hereford, England, grow their hair long because they don't know from one day to the next when they might have to go undercover. But then, they're the best. You can't be expected to compare."

"Why, you little shit," Makeev said in Russian, leaned

down to grab Dillon by the shirtfront and was promptly head-butted. He staggered back, and Billy put out a foot and tripped him, following it up with a kick in the ribs.

"Nice one," Billy said.

As Zorin picked his friend up, Greta jumped to her feet, furious. "Go to my cottage and wait for me. Now!" she added fiercely.

"Billy, you just can't get good help these days," Dillon said.

"I don't know what the world's coming to." Billy was smiling, but Greta wasn't.

"Damn you to hell, Dillon," and she turned and followed the other two down to the cottage area.

People had settled again, unfazed by a minor affray in a city where bombs and violence were part of their daily lives.

Parker said, "What in the hell was all that supposed to be about?"

"That, ould son, is the opposition, but I'll fill you in down at our cottage. Time to move out, Billy, not that we actually unpacked."

"It's all go with you."

As they went down the steps from the terrace, Dillon's Codex Four went. It was Sharif. "Mr. Dillon, Selim arrived a short while ago at the farm."

"We're on our way. Don't forget, half an hour and then call her."

"As we arranged."

Sharif switched off his mobile and stood there in the orange grove, aware of the smell, the lights of Ramalla Village over to his left, the farm beside the Tigris below, and felt strangely sad. Had he done the right thing? Who knew? It was in the hands of Allah now.

In their cottage, Dillon brought Parker up to speed and opened the hardware bag. He produced two Colt .25 semiautomatics in ankle holsters and gave one to Billy.

"A woman's gun," Parker said.

"Not with hollow-point cartridges. Put a Walther in your waistband behind your back, Billy." He smiled at Parker. "If anybody searching finds it, they think that's it."

"My God, what is this, the third Gulf War?"

So Dillon told him.

Afterward, Parker said, "I knew it was big when Robson briefed me, but this is something else."

"A totally black operation. That's the way we work. You can sign the Official Secrets Act later."

"Unless you'd prefer not to," Billy said.

"Get stuffed. Like I said, it's got a bit boring lately."

Dillon took an Uzi machine pistol from the bag. "There are two of these in here, so with your Browning, I'd say we're ready to rock and roll."

"Just one thing," Parker said. "Does all this mean you don't trust Sharif?"

"No—what it means is I don't trust anybody. So we

take the hardware bag, leave anything else, leave the lights on and the radio."

"And leave the bill at reception," Billy said.

"Naturally."

"I parked round the back. Ford station wagon."

"Then, as they say in the movies, let's get the show on the road," Dillon told him.

And some ten minutes later, Greta Novikova was in the middle of telling Zorin and Makeev exactly what she thought of them when her mobile went. It was Sharif.

"He's at Ramalla. Arrived a short while ago."

"Excellent. Zorin and Makeev are with me now."

"Do you want me to join you?"

"No, meet us there."

"Do you still intend to dispose of them?"

"Of course, that's the whole point of the exercise. Does it give you a problem?"

"Not at all."

"I'll see you later."

Sharif switched off his mobile, looked over at the farm beside the river for a moment, then walked down through the orange trees toward it.

Zorin drove, Makeev beside him, in a Jeep Cherokee, Greta sitting in the back. Makeev was checking out an AK-47 with a folding stock.

"This should do the job," he said, laughing, and

punched Zorin on the shoulder. "An easy one, this. Not like hunting that Iraqi general in Basra."

"You've worked for the Americans?" Greta asked.

"Good God, no. It was an honor killing. He'd raped somebody's wife in the Saddam days. The family wanted revenge."

"We hunted him down in a sewer," Zorin said. "The family wanted his manhood, but this fool got him with a stick grenade."

"So there wasn't much left of his manhood." Makeev laughed uproariously. "Not that you'd know much of that kind of thing sitting behind a GRU desk."

It occurred to her then that they were both on something and it wasn't drink. She was wearing a black crepe trouser suit, a purse in her lap. She put a hand inside and found what she sought, a Makarov. She fingered it, not nervous, just ready. She had killed on occasion, but these fools didn't know that.

"Oh, I don't know. There were sewers in Kabul. I was twenty-two years of age when the Mujahidin finally chased us out in ninety-two."

They had stopped laughing. "You were in Afghanistan?" Makeev sounded incredulous.

"Chechnya was worse. Now, *they* really were sewers." Zorin swerved to avoid a line of donkeys with produce for tomorrow's market, his headlights picking them out.

"Careful," she said severely. "We want to get there in one piece."

She took out a cigarette, lit it and sat back.

The run to Ramalla was smooth and took no more than fifty minutes. Dillon examined the map in the light of a flashlight as they got closer.

"I'd say pull in on the edge of the orange grove on the hill. That's not much more than a hundred yards away. You'll stay with the station wagon," he told Parker.

"And miss all the fun?"

"No, ride shotgun. I never take anything for granted, and there are night glasses in the bag." He lit a cigarette. "I've never trusted anyone or anything in my life. That's why I'm here."

Later, moving off the main road, Parker switched off the engine and coasted some distance down through the orange grove and halted. The farm lay below, a light in the windows. There were two or three boats passing down the Tigris toward Baghdad. It was extraordinarily peaceful.

"They came to Ramalla," Dillon said. "Very biblical."

"I'm not much on the Bible," Billy said.

"Well, I have the Irish attitude. There's nothing can happen in life that hasn't already happened in the Bible." He took two pairs of night glasses from the bag and gave one to Parker. "Take a look."

When he did himself, the house was plainly visible, with what looked like a barn on each side, one of them damaged, part of the roof gone. There was a parked Land Rover.

"That's the war for you," Dillon said and passed the glasses to Billy. "Notice the license plate on the Land Rover. It's Kuwaiti."

Billy passed them back. "So how do we do this?"

"We'll go down on foot. You take the Uzi and leave the other for the sergeant." He turned to Parker. "You've got the glasses. Monitor us."

"What for, exactly?"

"Who knows? Just do it. Come on, Billy," and he got out of the station wagon and started down the hill, Billy following.

They reached the damaged end of the farmhouse. Half the roof was gone, what had been double barn doors missing. It was dark inside, but Dillon took a chance and flicked on a small flashlight, revealing some rusting farm machinery. He switched off. "Not much here."

There was a sudden rattling on the part of the roof left intact and rain fell in an absolute downpour. "Christ," Billy said. "I thought this was Iraq."

"It rains in Iraq, Billy. Sometimes it rains like hell in Iraq."

He led the way along the front of the farmhouse and past the Land Rover. There were shutters at the windows, half closed, and Dillon peered in, Billy at his shoulder. They saw a living room with a large table, on which stood an oil lamp. There were chairs, a wooden sideboard, a fire of logs on a stone hearth. A radio was playing music softly, but there was no sign of anyone.

"We'll try the other barn," Dillon whispered and moved on.

There was a narrow window on each side of the barn door, and Dillon peered inside. "Well, there's your man, Billy. Take a look."

Inside, there were stalls for animals, and a large loft with bales of hay and reeds. There was also Selim in a shirt and jeans clearing out a stall with a rake.

Dillon said, "In we go."

He reached for the door handle and a donkey brayed at the back of the barn and several more answered, and that was strange, because at that time of night and in all that rain, why would they not be in the barn? But before he could react, the tailgate of the Land Rover swung open behind him and Sharif got out holding an AK-47. Two men in red-and-black-checked kaffiyehs over their faces got out behind him, also holding AKs. Dillon had started to turn, but the muzzle of Sharif's gun touched his back.

"I wouldn't, I really wouldn't. I have no desire to kill you, or you, Mr. Salter. Please pass the Uzi over."

"Fuck you," Billy said, but did as he was told.

"You should beware the Wrath of Allah, Mr. Salter."

"Jesus, you're one of them," Dillon said.

Sharif was searching them, found the two Walthers and passed them to his friends. "Actually, I'm not. I don't care about Al Qa'eda, or Wrath of Allah, or any of them. I'm not even a good Muslim. But I love my country. That's what's important to me, and I want you all to go away."

"Including the Russians."

"Especially the Russians. You think I want to see people like Belov getting their hands on our oil, running our country? I think not. Now, let's go inside and wait for Major Novikova and her friends. It'll be a nice surprise, I think."

He pulled open the door and Selim stopped raking and turned, startled and then relieved. "Major, you've got him."

"So it would seem, me ould son," Dillon told him. "If you're interested, Ashimov and Belov want you dead. I, on the other hand, can cut you a deal with Ferguson that could ensure your return to the delights of London."

They heard the sound of a car in the distance, and Sharif said, "Get ready to close the door a little." Two more men stood up behind hay bales above in the loft.

"On the other hand," Dillon said to Selim as one of the men pulled on the door, "maybe you want to stay down on the farm?"

A ll this had been seen by Parker through the night glasses as he stood by the station wagon. He reached for the Uzi and at the same moment heard the approach of the Cherokee and raised the night glasses again, tracking the Jeep as it descended from the main road to the farm. It slowed on the final run, and Makeev, clutching an AK, rolled out headfirst and darted through long grass to the rear of the barn. The Jeep came to a halt behind the Land Rover, Zorin and Greta Novikova got out, and at that moment, the door of the barn swung open and Sharif appeared with his friends. It was enough, and Parker started down the hill at a run.

Greta Novikova said to Sharif, "So you've betrayed us?"

"I've betrayed both sides. I've thought it over carefully and decided to become a patriot, which is what my four friends are. I spoke to them and they were happy to oblige."

"I think it would pay you to think again. Josef Belov has a long arm."

"Never mind that. What happened to Makeev?"

And Dillon, speculating, stuck his oar in. "That would be me. The bastard was rude to the lady on the terrace of the hotel, and I broke his nose for him." He smiled amiably. "Or something like that."

In fact, Makeev, at that moment, having gained access to the barn through a rear door, was mounting wooden steps to the entrance to the left, but his progress was awkward, the steps breaking away with some noise. One of the men in the loft appeared, cried out an alarm and fired, hitting Makeev in the chest, and Makeev shot him in return, then fell backward down the stairs.

Down below, Dillon nodded to Billy and they both pulled the Colts from their ankle holsters and confronted

Sharif and his men. Nobody fired. There was a kind of tableau, a frozen moment, the door swinging all the way back in the wind, rain driving in.

Sharif raised his AK. "I'm sorry, Mr. Dillon," and Parker appeared in the doorway and shot him twice.

What happened then was very fast, very quick. Dillon swung, threw himself at Greta, flinging her out of the way. "Get in one of the stalls," he cried, as bullets shredded the floor beside him from the loft. He turned, firing twice, and the man up there came down headfirst.

Billy had dodged into the shelter of a stall and picked off one man carefully, a bullet to the head, and shot the other in the back as he turned to run away.

There was silence, and then Parker walked in, soaked. "Jesus" was all he could say.

Selim cowered on hands and knees in one of the stalls, and Zorin had produced a pistol. Greta moved out into the open. "For God's sake, put it away. We've lost."

Sharif groaned and moved a little and Dillon dropped to one knee, not that there was much to be done. Sharif couldn't even manage a smile.

As Dillon stood up, Zorin moved in behind him and put his pistol to his back. "I've had enough for one night, so I'm leaving and taking this bastard with me." He glanced at Greta. "You want to come, get over here."

"As you say."

"I like that. Maybe I could teach you how to do as you're told."

She was very close to him. "But I always do." She

took out the Makarov, rammed it into his back and shot him twice. He went down like a stone.

"Now what?" Billy asked Dillon.

"Another bad night in Iraq, Billy. We get the hell out of here." He nodded to Parker. "You did well." He turned to Selim. "I could shoot you, but you'll do better with Ferguson. Stay here and you're a dead man one way or another when Ashimov hears you're on the loose." He turned to Greta. "Isn't that so, Major?"

"I'd have to agree."

"But you didn't shoot me, you shot your own man," Selim argued. "It makes no sense."

"Well, she's a woman." Dillon pushed him over to Parker. "Get him in the station wagon."

Parker took Selim away, a hand on his arm, and Dillon and Greta paused in the doorway, Billy watching, his Uzi back in his hands. Dillon gave her a cigarette, took one himself and lit them with his old Zippo.

"Give you a lift, lady?"

"I don't think so. I'll take the Cherokee, get back to the Al Bustan and pack. Next step for you is the airport, I imagine."

"Why did you do it?"

"Does it really matter? Let's say I liked you and I didn't like them, and Sharif, as it happened, screwed things up big-time."

"Yeah, but where's that leave you with Ashimov and Belov?" Billy demanded.

"Oh, I'll give a satisfactory version of events. I'm good at that, and there's no one to contradict me."

Dillon opened the door of the Cherokee and said, "In you go, girl." Which she did, and put down the window. He leaned in. "I owe you one. I owe you a life."

"That means a lot to an Arab, Dillon, but you're Irish and a bastard. A charming one, but that's what you are."

She switched on the engine. "Buy me a drink at the Dorchester sometime and we'll call it quits."

"It's a deal."

"One more thing." She smiled out at him. "I'm still on the other side."

"I never doubted it."

She drove away, and Billy said, "That's a hell of a woman."

"A one-off, Billy. Now let's get moving."

They started up to the orange grove and he took out his Codex Four and called Lacey. "We're on our way, plus the passenger I mentioned."

"No problem, Sean. I've spoken to Robson, so it was all in the security pipeline. I'll confirm it now. We'll be waiting. Was it rough?"

"You wouldn't want to know."

"That bad? Ah, well, see you soon."

Dillon took out his cigarettes and said to Selim, who sat between him and Billy, "Do you use these?"

Selim was trembling a little. "Not for years."

"Then have one now. It'll help settle your nerves. Stay here and Belov's people will get you one way or another, but you're too valuable to waste, which is why I'm taking you back to Ferguson. As I've told you, play ball and you'll be fine."

"But my roots are here."

"Bollocks," Billy said. "Look out there at the romance of Iraq. Bleeding peasants at this time of night in the pouring rain, leading donkeys for the morning market in Baghdad to make a few bob. It's a shithole."

"And you're British anyway," Dillon said. "Born in London, went to St. Paul's, Cambridge."

"You went to St. Paul's?" Billy said. "I didn't know that. I was there for two years. My uncle Harry wanted to make a gentleman of me."

Selim was interested in spite of himself. "What happened?"

"They expelled me when I was sixteen for beating up two prefects. I've never told anyone that before, not even you, Dillon."

"Well, there you go." Dillon smiled. "A great man once said England was a splendid, tolerant and noble country, and even though I'm Irish, I'd have to agree. Let's put it this way. There are mosques all over London."

The first thing Greta did at the cottage when she got back was to call and arrange an early-morning departure for the Falcon. Then she phoned Ashimov, finding him in bed, because in London it was three in the morning. He was all attention, sat up and reached for a cigarette.

"How's it going?"

"I'm on my way back, that's how it's going. Sharif sold us out."

"I'll have his balls for that, I promise."

"No need. They ambushed us at Ramalla—Dillon, Slater and Sharif. There was a firefight. Zorin and Makeev were killed. I managed to shoot Sharif and got away in the darkness. I saw Dillon, Salter and some other men take Selim away to a station wagon. I was close enough to hear Dillon say something like 'Let's get out of here. Next stop the airport.' I waited until they'd gone and came back to the house in the Jeep."

"It's like a black comedy," he said. "A total farce."

"I'm sure they're going to squeeze Selim dry in some London safe house," she said.

"Yes, I'll have to find out where that is. But at least you're safe, my love. I'll expect you tomorrow."

She put the phone down, quite pleased with herself, and went to bed.

A t Baghdad Airport, they gained access through a discreet security entrance, where Robson and Lacey waited in a Land Rover.

"Follow us, Sergeant, straight to the plane," Robson called.

They did and found the Citation waiting, ready to go. The two vehicles stopped at the bottom of the steps and they all got out.

Robson said, "Please board now, gentlemen. You've sort of never been here, if you follow me. Much better all round."

"You've got a good man here." Dillon turned and shook hands with Parker. "We'll do it again sometime."

"Once around the houses with you is enough for any man, but good luck."

Billy pushed Selim up the steps, Dillon followed and then Lacey, who closed the door. Selim sank into a seat. Lacey joined Parry in the cockpit.

Dillon took out his Codex Four and called Ferguson, as Greta had done with Ashimov, finding him in bed.

"Who in the hell is it at this time in the morning?"

"Dillon. Just leaving Baghdad Airport."

"Have you got him?"

"That we have."

"Was it bad?"

"Oh, the usual. Billy did well. Two more notches."

"And Novikova?"

"Still in one piece. Quite a girl, but I'll tell you later."

"Good man, Sean, we'll be waiting at Farley."

The Citation started along the runway, lifted and rose very quickly. Billy tilted his seat. "I'm for a nap," he said and closed his eyes.

Selim was shaking slightly, and Dillon opened one of the lockers, produced a blanket. "There you go, wrap yourself in that."

Selim said in a small voice, "Thank you, Mr. Dillon."

Dillon opened the bar box, found half a bottle of Bushmills whiskey and a glass, into which he poured a large one.

"That 'Committee for Racial Harmony' you've been

sitting on at the House of Commons, play your cards right and you could be back there before you know it, sitting on the Terrace by the Thames, with tea, cakes and cucumber sandwiches. Think about it."

He sat back and poured himself another whiskey.

LONDON

10

The Citation landed at Farley Field at ten in the morning, under gray skies and heavy rain, remarkably like Iraq. Ferguson waited in the Daimler, Hannah Bernstein standing beside it in a raincoat, an umbrella over her head. Behind them was a Land Rover containing two men in civilian clothes. They were, in fact, staff sergeants in the Royal Military Police, named Miller and Dalton, and they worked for Ferguson at the Holland Park safe house. As the Citation rocked to a halt, they got out of the car.

The door of the plane opened, the steps came down. Lacey came first, followed by Dillon, Selim behind him huddled in his blanket. Billy was next and then Parry. Ferguson went to greet them.

He said formally, "You are Dr. Ali Selim?"

"That's right." Selim seemed quite calm now.

Ferguson turned and said to Hannah, "Superintendent?"

There was a reluctance to her, but she said, "Under the Anti-Terrorism Act, you may be held indefinitely. Under the Official Secrets Act, you may not speak of it or why you are here."

"Am I not entitled to a lawyer?" Selim asked.

"No." Ferguson turned to the staff sergeants. "Deliver him to the safe house. Treat him well. Give him a change of clothes and whatever food he wants. Remember that he's a Muslim."

Hannah said, "I'd like to go with him, sir."

The military police were putting Selim in the rear of the Land Rover, and Ferguson took Hannah to one side. "I know you don't approve, my dear, but desperate situations require desperate remedies. However, we're not the Gestapo. We won't mistreat him. Now, off you go. I'll see you later."

She turned to Dillon, obviously unhappy. "Good to see you back, Sean."

Dillon felt sorry for her, but it was Billy who said, "Don't waste your sympathy, Superintendent. They'd have killed us, and they tried hard enough—even wanted to kill Selim. People like you, your conscience, your morality. Nothing's ever enough, is it?"

Dillon said, "Leave it, son," and she turned and got in the Land Rover and was driven away.

The rain suddenly increased. Billy said, "To hell with it. It's me for the Dark Man and a full English breakfast."

"An excellent idea." Ferguson turned to Lacey and Parry. "My thanks, gentlemen. We'll be seeing each other soon, I'm sure."

He got in the Daimler with Dillon and Billy and was driven away.

The Dark Man, like most London pubs these days, offered breakfast. Dora was on duty, greeted them with enthusiasm and vanished into the kitchen. The place was quiet, and they settled in a booth, and five minutes later, Harry burst in with Joe Baxter and Sam Hall. He embraced Billy in a bear hug.

"Jesus, that was quick."

"The way it happened, Harry," Dillon said.

Salter turned to his nephew. "What was it like, Baghdad?"

"Well, it wasn't like a Sinbad movie. It was pissing with rain most of the time. To be honest, Harry, I feel sorry for them."

"So you got Selim?"

Dillon glanced at Ferguson, who nodded. "You might as well tell him."

Which Dillon did, as Dora arrived with the breakfasts.

Afterward, Harry put an arm around Billy. "You young bastard, you've done it again."

"We were lucky this time," Billy told him. "Or at least Dillon was. If it hadn't been for Novikova, he'd have been a dead man. That Makeev creep was a bad sod."

"So what happens now?" Harry demanded.

"We'll put Selim into a safe house," Ferguson said. "We'll see what he's got to say."

"So you won't be standing him up at the Old Bailey?" Harry said. "For conspiracy in Mrs. Morgan's death?"

"It's pointless. We wouldn't get anywhere. What's far more important is information about what Selim's been up to with the Wrath of Allah."

"And how are you going to get that? This isn't the Algerian War and the French Foreign Legion. You're not going to wire up his bits and pieces to a car battery."

"There are more subtle ways."

"The Superintendent wasn't very happy," Billy said. "With all that Anti-Terrorism Act stuff and the fact that he doesn't get a lawyer."

"It can't be helped. As I said earlier, we live in difficult times. It is war to the knife. Things have changed. Speaking of which—you know about the Omega Program, Dillon?"

Harry said, "And what would that be?"

"It's an implant containing a computer chip that tracks a person's whereabouts. The Prime Minister and cabinet ministers each have one. He insisted I had it done last year. At the time, he didn't want it spread any further, but he's changed his mind since the attempt on Cazalet. He wants us to use every tool at our disposal, and he's authorized me to include anyone I think appropriate. So I'm insisting that you, Dillon and the Superintendent get it also. Major Roper's already got one." He gave Dillon a card. "Professor Henry Merriman, Harley Street. Nine o'clock tomorrow morning."

"Christ," Billy said. "Bionic man."

Harry burst into laughter. Ferguson said, "Not so fast, Billy. You've gotten yourself up to your neck in my affairs for some time now, and this particular situation is bad and getting worse. So under the circumstances, I think you'd better have one implanted, too."

It was Dillon's turn to laugh. "There goes your love life, Billy."

Billy did not look amused.

Ashimov was still at Drumore Place and arranged for a company car to pick Novikova up at Belfast Airport. Then he phoned Belov in Moscow and broke the bad news. Belov took it badly.

"Here I am up to my neck in difficult negotiations, and this kind of thing happens. It won't do, Yuri. I put you in charge, gave you unlimited discretion, total resources, unlimited money . . ."

"I'm sorry, Josef. Makeev and Zorin came highly recommended, they did good work in the past."

"And now they're dead, along with this Sharif and his four friends. The only one who comes out of it with any credit is Novikova. Dillon and this Salter boy are serious business."

"I agree."

"Then *deal* with them seriously. Enough messing

about. You tell me Kelly and Murphy knew him in the IRA? Fine. That means they'll know how he works. Tell them to get a crew together and to sort Ferguson's people out once and for all. Just get it done. I'm coming to Belfast myself. I had planned to return to London, but under the circumstances I think it's best I stay away, let them do their work. Don't fail me, Yuri."

Greta arrived soon afterward, and Yuri greeted her warmly. "Did you manage to get any sleep?"

"I had a couple of vodkas and crashed out for most of the trip."

"Good. We're driving down to the Royal George for lunch. I want you to meet Dermot Kelly and Tod Murphy."

They went out to the car. "What about Belov?"

"I've spoken to him."

"And?"

"He wants us to go to war. I'll explain as we go."

At the Royal George, they sat in a corner booth with Kelly and Murphy, enjoyed a shepherd's pie with Guinness and Greta gave her version of the events at Ramalla.

They found the whole thing very amusing, and it occurred to her, and not for the first time, that the Irish were not like other people. They never seemed to take anything seriously. It made her think of Dillon, and in a way that didn't sit comfortably with her.

"Jesus, but Sean's the one," Kelly said. "You've got to give it to the bastard."

"Mind you, this Billy Salter's close behind him," Tod Murphy said. "Maybe his mother was a Cork woman."

"No, that was Ferguson," Kelly said. "She was a Cork woman. It's a known fact."

It was Greta, exasperated, who said, "Well, if you've finished exploring the niceties of Irish family relationships, could we decide exactly what you intend to do?"

"Oh, Tod's the planning genius when you can get his nose out of a book," Kelly told her.

"We'll get together some of the old outfit," Tod said. "Me and Dermot and two others. That will be enough."

"For Dillon and Salter? I wonder."

"How will you travel?" Ashimov asked.

"There's a fella I know called Smith who runs air taxis, not far from here. He's been doing illegal flights for years. Goes in under six hundred feet, so he's not on the radar. Has a Navajo twin-engine job that'll do six. There are still old World War Two airstrips here and there, where the local farmer looks the other way if there's enough money in the envelope. Saves going through security, and we can take the right hardware."

"And where will you stay, in Kilburn?" Ashimov asked, naming the most Irish borough in London, virtually a ghetto.

"If there's ever a hint of IRA trouble, Scotland Yard makes straight for Kilburn," Kelly said. "We've got contacts that could help, but it's best to keep out of there. In fact, we'll try Indian territory." He glanced at Murphy. "China Wharf?"

"Perfect."

"That's in Wapping," Kelly said. "It's an old tea warehouse owned by Tod's aunt Molly. She married an Englishman named Harris. Special Branch never knew about her. She turned it into a lodging house years ago. We used to use it as a bolt-hole in London."

"She's a widow lady of eighty-three," Tod said. "Can't be bothered anymore, so she lives on the ground floor and leaves the other rooms empty."

"Sounds good to me." Ashimov got up. "You sort it all out. Move when you want to. Meanwhile, Greta will research where Ferguson keeps his safe houses."

"Fine by us," Kelly said.

"Good."

Afterward, Yuri and Greta walked down toward the pier. "It's beautiful," she said, as they looked over the tiny harbor.

"There's not much going on these days. Only half a dozen fishing boats, and they're out at the moment. The boat at the end of the pier is Dermot's, the *Kathleen*. He's had her for years. She's his pride and joy."

It was a thirty-foot cabin cruiser, shabby, with paint peeling, and Greta said, "It doesn't look like much."

"It sn't meant to, but it's got twin screws, radar, automatic steering and a depth sounder. Everything you need for an illegal passage by night, plus thirty knots."

He lit a cigarette. "Come on. I'll show you the rest of the estate and then it's back to London."

Jake Cazalet was sitting at his desk in the Oval Office signing papers when Blake Johnson came in.

"I've just had Charles Ferguson on the line, Mr. President. Dillon seems to have come through big-time."

"Tell me."

Blake did, and afterward, the President said, "The man never ceases to amaze me. So what happens now?"

"Ferguson will squeeze Selim dry if he can. Any leads they can prise out of him could prove invaluable."

"You don't need to tell me."

"Naturally, they'll pass all the relevant information on to us."

"I'd expect them to. In this, Blake, we must rely on Ferguson. Selim is a British citizen." He sighed and shook his head. "My God, the times we live in." He smiled suddenly. "I shouldn't think Josef Belov's too happy about all this."

"I shouldn't imagine he is, sir," and Blake went out.

On a quiet side road in Holland Park stood an Edwardian town house in the middle of about an acre of gardens surrounded by high walls. A sign at the electronic gate said PINE GROVES NURSING HOME. It was, in fact, Ferguson's safe house.

Hannah, Miller and Dillon delivered Selim there, and

were admitted by military police wearing a kind of uniform of navy blue blazers and flannel slacks.

Selim said, "Nursing home?"

"We have medical facilities," said Dillon. "So it's not a total lie. Don't be deceived by appearances. Security is everything here. The police may not be in army uniform, but they're all armed. There are no bars, but the windows are electrically wired. This is a fortress, Doctor Selim. Resign yourself to that. Now Sergeant Dalton will show you to your room. We'll talk later."

Selim was amazed at his treatment. The room was decent, with a window overlooking the garden. A selection of clothes was available in the drawers and a closet. He showered and changed, then Miller took him down to a sitting room of sorts with a table, chairs, a gas fire and a mirror.

Dalton said, "We're aware of your food requirements, so the chef has prepared a special meal." The door opened and Miller came in with a tray, which he placed on the table. "If there's anything unsatisfactory, please say so, sir."

"No, this is fine." Selim sat down and started to eat. "I would appreciate some tea."

Which was provided and he continued to eat, and on the other side of the mirror, Ferguson, Dillon, Hannah and Roper watched, waiting until he had finished. Miller reappeared and took away the tray. Dalton waited, watchful.

Selim raised his voice. "If you are there behind the

mirror, General Ferguson, do come in now. Whatever else I may be, I'm not a fool."

Dillon grinned at the General.

"Right, in we go, people," Ferguson said, and led the way.

Ferguson nodded to Dalton. "If you'd go into the other room and observe, I'd appreciate it."

"Certainly, sir."

Roper maneuvered his wheelchair, as Hannah and Ferguson sat down. Dillon sat on the windowsill, smoking a cigarette.

"To clarify things," Ferguson said, "I'm responsible for the Prime Minister's personal security system. I have no connection with the other security services. I have carte blanche on behalf of the Prime Minister to operate as I see fit. Detective Superintendent Bernstein is my assistant, on loan from Special Branch at Scotland Yard."

"And Mr. Dillon? I know what Mr. Dillon does. He kills people."

"And Wrath of Allah doesn't?" Dillon asked.

"Superintendent, I appeal to you. Why am I denied a lawyer? Is this just?"

Hannah had trouble with that and it showed. She turned to Ferguson. "Sir, perhaps . . ."

"Perhaps nothing. Major Roper, why don't you begin?"

Roper said, "I've prepared a report, Dr. Selim. It details your relationship to Henry Morgan, and, of course, his intention to assassinate the President of the United States. It outlines the suspicious death of his mother. It makes clear the basic links between these two and the Queen Street Mosque, as well as your relationship with Yuri Ashimov and, through him, Josef Belov."

"None of this can be proven," Selim said, but his voice was subdued.

"There's little doubt that there has been a trade in young British Muslims, recruited for terrorist camps originally in Iraq, now in various Muslim countries. I have in my possession considerable confidential information regarding the traffic between the Belov organization and you, acting as a front man for a number of so-called charities."

"All of it perfectly legitimate," Selim said weakly. "Anything else is a lie."

"Many donations to the Children's Trust in Beirut."

"All for charitable works, education."

"Charitable? The Children's Trust is a front of Hizbollah. That's well known. Both the Marxist League and Free the People have links with Al Qa'eda. The Children's Trust in Iraq is simply another way of saying Party of God, one of the most militant terror groups."

"None of this can be proved." Selim was desperate now. "All the trusts, the educational groups, any payments by me on the Belov company's behalf were made in good faith. You can't say otherwise. Mr. Belov paid for our building work at Queen Street, even the new school."

"I have a list of organizations you've passed money to," Roper said. "It's a fact."

"I'm running out of patience," Ferguson told him. "I'm the first to agree that we stand very little chance of bringing Belov to a courtroom. He's too rich, too powerful, and he's covered his back too well. What I want from you are details of the camps, the lists of organizations, names and addresses. Do that properly and you'll be let off the hook. Slate clean."

"I can't," Selim said weakly.

"All right. If that's the way it is, then I'll have you flown back to Iraq, or Saudi Arabia, if you like. We'll dump you, then spread the word that you talked. If you're lucky, Belov's people will get to you first. A bullet would be preferable to being skinned alive by your own people, don't you think?"

Selim jumped up. "No, I beg you."

"Think about it, Selim. Think hard. I'll give you a little time. Come along, people," and he led the way out.

In the other room, Ferguson said to Dalton, "Keep a close eye on him, Sergeant. Anything comes up, phone me. Otherwise we'll speak tomorrow."

"Fine, sir." Dalton went out.

Ferguson said to the others, "Any questions?"

Roper said, "I'll get back to my computers, sir. Miller can take me in the van."

"I'll go with you," Dillon said. "You can drop me off."

Hannah said, "I have to confess I still don't find this easy, sir, his lack of legal representation."

"You think we're infringing on his human rights, Superintendent?"

"I suppose so."

"Well, in the circumstances in which we find ourselves, I'm not very interested in such a viewpoint. Does this mean that you would prefer to return to your normal duties at Scotland Yard?"

She hesitated. "You make it hard for me, sir."

"I have to. But I'll give you an option. Tomorrow morning, when you go to Harley Street to see Merriman to have the Omega implant, I suggest you visit the Reverend Susan Haden-Taylor at St. Paul's Church. You may recall I put Dillon in touch with her last year when I wanted his head cleared after the Rashid affair."

"And you think she could help?"

"She's a priest of the Church of England, as well as a top psychiatrist," Dillon said. "But most important, she's a truly good human being and she certainly helped me."

Hannah took a deep breath. "Fine. I'll do that," and she went out.

Dillon walked behind Roper's chair with Ferguson. "You can be a hard ould bastard, Charles."

"It's a hard ould world, Sean, and getting harder."

They stood and watched Roper wheel up the ramp into the back of the van. Miller raised the ramp and closed the door and Dillon called, "Wait for me." He turned to Ferguson. "Are we winning, Charles?"

"God knows, but as I've said before, we won't if we just play patty-cake," and Ferguson got in the Daimler and was driven away.

Dillon got in the rear of the van beside Roper's chair. "Well?" he demanded. "What do you think?"

Roper's eyes were dark in the ravaged, burned face. "Don't ask me, Sean. I'm what's left over after a car bomb."

About ten miles from Drumore Place, Tod Murphy turned the Land Rover into a narrow lane and came to a couple of hangars, a decaying control tower and a crumbling tarmac runway. If ever a place looked run-down, it was this, but then World War Two and the days when it had been used to patrol the Irish borders had been over for a long time. A single-engine Archer stood outside one of the hangars; the doors of the other stood open, revealing a twin-engine Navajo. The door of the Nissen hut opened and a man in old black flying overalls appeared: Ted Smith, around fifty, balding slightly and, like many pilots, rather small.

"Is it yourself, Tod?"

"Who else would it be, you daft bugger? Is the Navajo up and running?"

"First class. You fancy a day out?"

"You could say that. Four of us. Me, Dermot and two of the boys, Fahy and Regan."

"What for? A day's fishing over the border?"

"Farther than that. That place we used to go in the old days before the bloody Peace Process. Dunkley. The one that was a Lancaster bomber station in the war."

Smith's face dropped. "Jesus, Tod, not that again. I thought those days were behind us."

"You'll do as you're told and you'll be well taken care of. But if you say no, Dermot is likely to take care of you permanently. You follow?" He laughed and slapped Smith on the shoulder. "Don't look so worried. A quick one, Ted, just like the old days. In and out. You'll be away before you know it."

"Jesus, Tod, I don't know. I'm getting old for that sort of jig."

Tod took an envelope from his inside pocket and offered it to him. "Two thousand quid to seal the bargain, just to be going on with. We'll leave early in the morning. When we want to come back, I'll phone you. There'll be a big, big payday at the end of it, and just for dropping us onto a very old airfield in Kent, miles from anywhere."

As usual, greed won the day, and Smith took the envelope. "All right, I'll do it, Tod. Seven-thirty in the morning."

"Good man, yourself. I'll see you then," and Tod got back into the Land Rover.

Damn the IRA, but what could he do? Smith turned and went back into the Nissen hut.

A nd at half past seven the following morning, the Navajo, fully loaded, took off in spite of Smith's reluctance.

"There's a lot of bad weather out there, a front moving in over the Irish Sea."

"Then we'll rely on the ham sandwiches and good

Irish whiskey to keep our spirits up," Dermot told him. "Jesus, Tod, we've done this run at night in the old days and black as the hob of hell, so let's get on with it."

Which they did, and the whiskey flowed as the Navajo was pushed by a fierce tailwind over the Irish Sea, dampening the spirits of Kelly's men. They crossed the English coast over Morecambe. It was raining even harder now, a front advancing as they turned down toward the south country.

As Smith adjusted his course, Kelly, sitting beside him, said, "Everything okay?"

"It should start to quiet down. If it doesn't, we could always turn back."

"You wouldn't want to do that. Then I'd have to break your legs, wouldn't I?" Dermot smiled, looking terrible. "Just get on with it," and he got up and joined the others in the cabin.

It was raining in London, too, a short time later, as Billy got out of a cab at Professor Merriman's office in Harley Street and went inside. Dillon and Hannah Bernstein were already in Reception.

The young nurse behind the desk said, "Who's first?"

"That'll be me," Hannah told her. "I've got another appointment."

"Then follow me, please."

In his office, Merriman greeted her warmly while the nurse busied herself with items on a side table.

"It only takes a moment, Superintendent, but you'll have to remove your blouse. You can keep your bra on. I only need an armpit."

"Will it hurt?" Hannah asked as she took off her blouse.

"Not with this. An excellent anesthetic." The nurse handed him a plastic ampule. There was a slight prick on her arm and the skin went numb. "It's instant," he said, and the nurse handed him a sort of aluminum pistol. He placed the muzzle into her right armpit and pulled the trigger. She didn't feel a thing.

"Is that it?" she asked, as she pulled her blouse on.

"Absolutely. Your implant is already code indexed into the Omega computer. Where you go, it goes."

"I'm not sure I'm happy about that."

"It's a tool, Superintendent, that's all. A reflection of the world we live in."

She pulled on her jacket and coat. "That's one way of looking at it," she said. "Tell me, St. Paul's Church is near here, I believe?"

"End of the street and turn left."

"Thank you and good morning."

She went out and was followed by the nurse, who called Billy in. Dillon stood up.

"On your way already?"

"I have an appointment."

"At St. Paul's. She's a remarkable lady and good at extracting confessions. I should know."

"I'll see you later, then, back at the office."

She left, and Billy emerged. "No big deal."

"Good. I hate needles."

Billy said, "I'll see you later. I've got a bit of business back at the Dark Man."

"You're an idiot, Billy. Smuggled cigarettes from Amsterdam and you don't even need the money. You'll be back behind bars at Wandsworth."

"That'll be the day," Billy said and left.

When Dillon emerged into Harley Street, it was still raining. He lit a cigarette, looked down the pavement in the direction Hannah had gone and walked the same way. St. Paul's Church was on the other side of the street when he turned the corner, a notice board in front with the times of services and the name of the priest. He went up the steps, eased open the small Judas gate in the main door and stepped inside.

It was Victorian, a half-dark sort of place, and there was the smell of damp, candles and incense. He noticed a statue of the Virgin and Child, more candles flickering there, all very old-fashioned Church of England, except for the newer fashion that allowed women priests.

Susan Haden-Taylor was a calm, pleasant woman in a clerical collar and cassock. She was sitting on the opposite side of the aisle from Hannah, two pews away, but facing her.

"Yes," she was saying. "Charles Ferguson has spoken to me of your dilemma. And his."

"And his?" Hannah was astonished and showed it.

"Yes. There are always two sides to everything, however

simplistic that may sound. Charles tells me you read psychology at Cambridge."

"That's right."

"And that your father is Arnold Bernstein. I know his work. One of the finest general surgeons in London."

"And my grandfather is Rabbi Julian Bernstein."

"Leaving you totally walled in by morality."

"Something like that."

At the back of the church, Dillon sat on a chair behind a pillar in the corner and listened.

"During my time with the police," said Hannah, "I've killed when I had no choice and I've been wounded myself. I even killed a woman once, a truly evil person who was trying to kill a friend. I could accept all this as somehow being part of the job."

"So what is the problem now? You know you can speak freely. As both a priest and a psychiatrist, I must keep your confidence."

Hannah told her. When she was done, Susan Haden-Taylor said, "I'm not taking sides, just examining the situation. In spite of what he's been responsible for, you want Selim to have a legal representative, which means due process of law and an eventual trial, which will probably take six months to come to court, if not longer."

"I know all the difficulties."

"Whereas Ferguson wants the details of all those who've passed through this Wrath of Allah organization before they have time to set more bombs off. In pursuit of that aim, he obviously feels that giving Selim a hard time is worth it. Don't you?"

"Dammit." Hannah was extremely frustrated. "It makes me sound so bloody unreasonable. I've been raised on the law, I believe in the law. It's all we've got."

"So do I, but the times are changing very rapidly and we must face that. Global terrorism provides a whole new perspective. It's not that you're wrong, Hannah, but it's not that Ferguson is wrong either. And one final point. As in all things, each of us has personal choice."

"Which means?"

"If you really feel strongly about this matter, it would be better if you resigned. Better for yourself. In fact, better for everyone."

"How strange," Hannah said. "That makes me feel as if I'd be running away."

"It's the best I can do, I'm afraid. Can I offer you a cup of tea?"

"No, thanks, I'd better get on."

Dillon got up at once and slipped out through the Judas gate, where he lit a cigarette and stood waiting. She came out a few minutes later.

"What are you doing here?"

"Oh, I thought I'd hang around outside and see how you got on."

"You were right. She is a remarkable woman."

They started along Harley Street. "Are you still with us, then?"

"I suppose so. I'll give it another week or two and see. As I was leaving, she said the strangest thing."

"And what was that?"

"That when Christ told us to turn the other cheek, he

didn't tell us to do it twice. What on earth is that supposed to mean?"

Dillon grinned. "It makes perfect sense to me," and he hailed a cab.

At Dunkley in Kent, the visibility was poor in the pouring rain as Smith eased the Navajo down on the old decaying bomber runway and rolled to a halt by the decrepit hangars. A white Ford Transit was parked nearby, a man in a cloth cap and bomber jacket holding an umbrella.

Tod got the door open and they all piled out with their bags. Smith peered out, and Kelly said, "Keep your mobile with you at all times. When I call, you come running."

"You can rely on me, Dermot, but I'm best out of it now."

He closed the door, went into the cockpit and took off fast a moment later. Dermot led the way to the Transit, holding out his hand.

"So you came yourself, Danny." He turned to Fahy and Regan. "Danny Malone. Runs the best pub in Kilburn, the Green Man, and a good friend from the great days."

"Sure, and I thought I'd come myself, Dermot." They got in and he climbed behind the wheel. "And I've spoken to your aunt Molly about China Wharf, only she isn't there, Dermot. She's spending time at Brighton with an old friend."

"Well, that's a damn shame," Tod put in.

"No trouble. She told me where a key was hidden and I checked and it was there. I've been to the supermarket, stocked you up with provisions. You'll be as right as rain. The job? Is it big?"

"When the time's right," Kelly said. "Dillon's involved. That's all you need to know. Maybe we'll get him this time."

At the Ministry of Defence, Hannah knocked on the door of Ferguson's office and went in, followed by Dillon. Ferguson, at his desk, looked up and sat back.

"So you're both part of Omega now. We should form a club."

"A very exclusive one, sir," Hannah said.

"Did you see Susan Haden-Taylor?" She nodded. "And what did she think?"

"What did you expect her to think?" Dillon said. "That difficult decisions are the privilege of rank whereas we, the poor bloody foot soldiers, just pull the trigger?"

"Oh, shut up for once, Dillon," Ferguson told him. "Have you made any decision yet, Superintendent?"

"If I could think it over for a week or so, sir, I'll soldier on."

The phone rang, he picked it up. "Ferguson." Suddenly he smiled. "Excellent. I'll be with you shortly." He put the phone down. "It looks like you'll have to, Superintendent. That was Dalton. Selim wants to see me. You'd both better come along."

China Wharf was a relic of the old tea clipper days, but times had changed and most of the warehouses were developed or boarded up and awaiting their turn. Danny Malone unlocked the door and led the way in, followed by the others. There was a large sitting room, all the furniture old-fashioned, a kitchen on the same scale. He put the key on the table.

"Two bedrooms and a bathroom down the hall, five bedrooms and two bathrooms upstairs from when it was a lodging house."

"It'll be fine," Kelly said, and turned to Tod. "I'll phone Ashimov and let him know we made it. Then we'll get together with him and Novikova, see what she's got." He rubbed his hands together. "Now bacon and eggs, a good old fry-up, sounds good to me. But who's going to cook it, that's the thing."

"Well, not me," Danny Malone said. "I'll be off now. You let me know if there's anything else I can do," and he went out.

At Holland Park, they stood with Miller and looked through the false mirror. Selim sat at the table drinking tea, while Dalton sat on the other side and they chatted.

"You are a very reasonable man, Mr. Dalton," Selim was saying.

Miller said, "Fred's done a really good job on him, General. I actually think he's about ready to see reason."

"Then in we go," and Ferguson led the way.

Selim and Dalton stopped talking and Dalton stood up, but Selim remained seated. "You wanted to see me," Ferguson said. "Do I assume you're going to be sensible?"

"General, I know you are not the Gestapo. You won't wire up my extremities, or inject me with succinyl-choline or put me in a bath of water until I nearly drown. It isn't the British way. But I do know that you will sentence me to death if, as you have threatened, you return me to Iraq or anywhere else in the Middle East."

"So what is your decision?"

"I'm a contemptible coward who believed in my mission but is quite simply afraid to die. As you rightly point out, it would be slow and painful. So, yes, I will co-operate."

"Fine." Ferguson stayed calm. "But you must tell me everything, and I do mean everything. Not only the names of the wretched young men drawn into your world of violence, but the identities of your sponsors, the moneymen, the Belovs."

Selim was just as calm. "You can never touch Belov. He's much too powerful."

"That may be true, but we can damn well try."

"Good luck to you. However, I do have terms."

"Terms?" Ferguson frowned.

"Certainly. I will deal only with you. I will talk only with you. Mr. Dillon may have saved my life in Iraq, but he killed friends of mine while doing it. I respect Superintendent Bernstein, but she is Jewish and it would not be seemly. The sergeants have treated me decently, so I have no objection to them. However, I don't like this place." He shook his head. "I really don't like it at all. We are in the middle of London. There are too many of my brothers around here, too many people who would surely try to kill me if they knew I was here, no matter how good the security is. Is there somewhere else we could go?"

"Jesus, son, you don't want much," Dillon said.

Hannah turned to Ferguson. "Huntley Hall, sir. It's away from here, and the security's just as good."

"That's true. Roper could come down and handle the technical stuff."

"No," Selim said. "I said only you, and I meant it."

"I shouldn't think that would be a problem, sir," Hannah said. "Roper could handle it by remote. He's done it before."

Selim said, "Huntley Hall?"

"It's a lovely old house in St. Leonard's Forest near Horsham, about an hour and a half from London. It used to be Lord Faversham's place. When he died, he left it to the nation. There's lots of woodland. Excellent pheasant shooting."

"And now you've turned it into the kind of place where the only things that get shot are intruders?"

Dillon laughed. "You'll love it."

Ferguson stood up and said to Dalton and Miller, "Get him ready. I'll go home and pack. When I return, we'll drive down to Huntley. Be prepared to stay for as long as it takes. Dr. Selim, I'll see you later."

They took him out and Ferguson turned to Dillon and Hannah. "It's something of a surprise, but I'll take it as far as I can. You're in charge here, Superintendent."

"Very well, sir. You can rely on me."

"And you," Ferguson said. "Try to behave yourself."

"Don't I always?" Dillon said.

"That'll be the day," Ferguson said and led the way out.

I t was approximately an hour and a half later that he returned, this time in a cab, bag in hand. Fifteen minutes later, the Land Rover emerged, Miller and Dalton in the front, Ferguson and Selim in the rear.

A few yards down the road a Telecom van was parked, a manhole cover was up and a man in helmet and yellow jacket was working. He had a clear look as the Land Rover went by and spoke into a small mike in Russian.

"Land Rover just coming your way now. Two in the front. Ferguson and Selim in the rear. Stick to them like glue. I'll notify Major Novikova."

The Land Rover paused at the end of the one-way street, then turned into the main road. A motorcycle, ridden by a man in black leather, emerged from a side street and took up station, staying well back.

11

At China Wharf, while Fahy and Regan did the cooking, Kelly contacted Ashimov. "So here we are. What next?"

"We'll come round and see you to discuss that. Greta did some research in her GRU files and discovered that Ferguson has a safe house in Holland Park."

"Well, that's useful. Is Selim there?"

"I'd be amazed if he wasn't. Just to make sure, though, she's got a couple of her people from the embassy on watch there, posing as workmen. I'll let you know what they find out."

He drove to the embassy, and found Greta in her office, putting papers into her briefcase. She looked flushed and excited.

"It marches, Yuri. It marches. Not only was Selim definitely in the safe house, he's now left. He was seated with Ferguson behind two men in a Land Rover. It's definite."

"So where were they going?"

"I don't know, but my number-two man, a young lieutenant called Ivanov, is on their trail on a motorcycle."

"Is he any good?"

"Excellent. They won't give him the slip, even if they try."

"Then while we're waiting to hear what he comes up with, let's go visit those Irish clods at China Wharf."

The Land Rover moved south out of London through heavy traffic to Leatherhead, then onward to Dorking, stopping on the other side for fuel. It was busy, with plenty of cars around, and Ivanov was able to be unobtrusive. He called Greta just as she was arriving at China Wharf with Ashimov. He told her where he was. "The main road leads to Horsham. Does that make any sense?"

"Plenty. I think you may find a village near there named Huntley. Stay with it and call me back."

"Huntley?" Ashimov said.

"Ferguson's other safe house." She held up her briefcase. "It's all in here."

"Good. Then let's go in."

The road to St. Leonard's Forest passed through impressive woodland, but was not very busy, only the occasional car and the odd farm vehicle. Ivanov stayed way back, allowing anything that came to overtake him. The road was comparatively straight and he was able to keep the Land Rover in view far up front.

In the end, he had luck, but you always needed that. A large agricultural container truck came up behind him, and he pulled over to let it pass. It provided perfect cover for another couple of miles and he stayed well back, looking beyond it until he saw the Land Rover turn off the road. He slowed, taking his time, allowing the truck to move on, and came to high walls topped by what, to his practiced eye, looked like an electronic fence. There was a gate, obviously also electronic, a small lodge and a sign that said HUNTLEY HALL INSTITUTION.

He kept on going. The walls extended for about a quarter of a mile, the grounds heavily wooded. He had a glimpse of the roof of a large house in the distance, no more, and then he came to the village of Huntley itself—very English, very traditional, cottages scattered on the main street, a stone bridge over a brook, a village store, a fuel station and a pub called the Huntley Arms.

He stopped for fuel, and a young woman served him. His English was perfect, which was how he had been trained. "I seemed to get lost in Horsham. I wanted to cut across to the Brighton Road."

"Keep going, you'll come to the A Twenty-three and that'll take you all the way down to Brighton."

"This is certainly an out-of-the-way place."

"That's true. Nothing much happens here."

He followed her to the kiosk and got his money

out. "What was that place I passed, Huntley Park Institution?"

"Some sort of medical outfit. People in rehab, or that sort of thing. I wouldn't know, really. They keep to themselves."

He noticed there were a dozen trailers scattered in the woodland at the back of the garage.

"Who do you rent those to?"

"Nobody's staying now. Bird-watchers sometimes, people down for the shooting. We get quite busy in the summer."

"I like this place," he said. "Give me a card," which she did, and he added, "While I'm here, I might as well have something to eat. Is the pub any good?"

"It's all right. Pies, sandwiches, that sort of thing. You won't find anyone in there now except my granddad. He's got nothing better to do than drink beer with no one staying in the trailers."

He gave her a dazzling smile. "I'll give it a go."

She was right, for when he went in the pub it was exactly what he would have expected. A stone-flagged floor, an oaken bar backed by bottles, a beamed ceiling, about twenty empty tables and a log fire on an open hearth. An old man in a padded jacket and tweed cap was seated by the fire drinking a pint of beer.

A middle-aged woman appeared from somewhere at the back of the bar, drying her hands. "Can I help you, sir?"

"Took the wrong road from Horsham and lost my way. I'll have a beer, just one since I'm driving, and maybe you could find me a cheese sandwich. The young lady at the garage suggested I come in."

"That would be Betty."

"My granddaughter," the old man called. "Harold Laker's my name."

"Maybe I could buy you a beer," Ivanov said.

"A pint of bitter wouldn't be a burden."

"The old scrounger." The woman smiled. "Go on, you join him and I'll bring your drinks and the sandwiches."

H arold Laker was eighty years old and boasted of it. He'd been born on a local farm, worked all his life in the village, and he demolished a pint and accepted another as Ivanov kept him talking.

"Of course, it wasn't just the farming in the old days. There was the fishing, the foxhunting, though that's long gone. The shooting's really the only big thing left in season."

"What kind of birds?"

"All kinds. Good pheasant, especially on the estate when Lord Faversham was alive. I used to carry his guns, load for him. Wonderful wildlife on the estate. Rabbits, hares. Not these days, mind you."

"Why not?"

"Well, when he died, he left it to the nation, and the

powers that be turned it into some sort of medical institution."

"I noticed it when I was driving in. What goes on in there?"

"Nobody really knows, but they do say it's for people with head problems. Never see any of them round here, mind you." He sighed. "It was a poacher's paradise, that estate."

"I suppose you had your share, but not now with all that security. Electric fences, cameras at the gate."

"And inside the grounds."

"Really? And how would you know that?"

"Well, let's just say if I want a bird or two or a hare or a nice pheasant, I know where to go."

"You amaze me."

The old man patted the side of his nose with his finger. "Mum's the word. You don't always need to go over a fence."

There was cunning in his eyes, and Ivanov laughed.

"You old devil. You obviously know what other people don't." He rose. "Well, I must be away. It's been great talking to you, Mr. Laker." He went to the counter and paid his bill. "And give him another pint."

"He can talk the hind leg off a donkey," she said.

"Oh, he's all right. Reminds me of my grandfather. You never know what you can learn!"

When he rode away, he took the road back to Horsham, slowing to have another look at the gates as he went past Huntley Hall. About four miles farther on, he turned into a nice quiet turnoff in some trees and called Greta Novikova, who was seated at the sitting-room table at China Wharf with Ashimov and the four Irishmen, various documents spread in front of her.

"Ivanov. What have you got for me?"

"Ferguson has definitely taken Selim to Huntley Hall, but there's a lot more to it than that. Shall I leave it until I get back to London?"

"No, I want it now. Just let me plug in my recorder."

When he was finished, she cut in, the recorder still on.

"What do you think?"

"About Harold Laker? He's like my grandfather in Ukraine. A cunning old peasant. If you want my opinion, he's known that estate all his life and he poaches it to suit himself."

"But how? With all that security?"

"All I know is, the old bugger said when he needed a bird or two, or a rabbit or a hare, he knew where to go and, I quote, 'You don't always need to go over a fence.'"

"He's got a way in," she said, and there was awe in her voice.

"I'd say so."

"You've done well. Come home, Sergei."

She hung up and turned to Ashimov. "What do you think?"

"We'll have to send one of these lads for a little chat with Mr. Laker. But first things first. Let's have a look at those plans you showed us, Greta."

She laid them out, Huntley Hall quite plain, and the rolling areas of woodland. "You can see where there are

CCTV cameras and electronic devices in the trees at certain points. Mind you, these plans aren't perfect."

"Why not?" Kelly demanded.

"Because they're based on memory. Five years ago, we had a British spy called Sharkey in our hands in Moscow, and an exchange was arranged for one of our men, Orlov, who was being held at Huntley Hall. On the odd occasion, he was allowed out for a walk in the grounds and picked up a certain amount of visual information."

Tod said, "Sounds risky. Then I'm inclined to go with what Ivanov's said. The old man has a way in. I think Kelly and I should go down there in the morning. We'll put up at this trailer site Ivanov mentioned, get to know the old boy and find out his secret."

"By breaking his fingers?"

"Oh, you always want to do things the hard way, Dermot. No, three bottles of Bushmills should do it, and he'll turn out to be as greedy as people like him usually are." He turned to Greta. "Ivanov didn't sound Russian, what I heard. Does he have any kind of accent?"

"No, he was picked out because his mother was English."

"Right, so he's your English nephew, Dermot, who told you about the place. That's why we're calling in on our way to London from Brighton."

It was Ashimov who said, "Sounds good to me, but let's take it a step further. If in some way you can gain access to the grounds, what's the next move?"

"There isn't one," Tod said. "Not in advance. If he's taken out for a walk when we're around, we'll shoot him."

"And if not?"

"We'll handle things the way the cards fall."

There was silence, then Fahy said, "What about us?"

"You'll keep your eye on Major Roper. You've got all his details you need," Tod said. "Even you can't miss a bionic man in a wheelchair."

"Do we waste him if we get the chance?" Regan demanded.

"No. You wait to hear how we fare with Ferguson and Selim."

"And Dillon?" Fahy asked.

"You could try," Greta said and pushed some papers over to them. "That's his cottage in Stable Mews and a recent photo of him. Also his Mini car and its number."

Tod laughed. "Did you itemize his body count?"

"I didn't want to frighten anyone off." She pushed some other papers over. "Dillon's friends, the Salters. The young one is as bad as Dillon and his uncle was one of the biggest gangsters in London in his time, so be warned."

"If the need for any extras arises while we're away," she went on, "a car or something like that, you call Danny Malone. He'll fix you up. He used to be a supplier for the Provos."

"The only one left is Bernstein, the Special Branch Superintendent."

"Huh," Fahy said. "I'm not worried about her. Woman coppers should stick to desk work."

"I wouldn't be so sure. It says here that she shot dead a woman, a leading Loyalist hard-liner named Norah Bell," Greta pointed out.

"And wasn't she the original bitch from hell, Protestant or not?" Dermot said.

Tod smiled. "Well, we've all got our wicked ways. Norah's were just a little bit more wicked than most. Is that it, then?"

"I'd say so. We'll keep an eye on Bernstein," Greta said. She put her papers in her briefcase, got up and asked Ashimov, "Shall we go?"

"I think so." He nodded casually to the others. "Stay in touch at all times."

"We have all your mobile numbers, so if we don't hear from you, you'll be hearing from us."

As she and Ashimov went to the door, Tod said, "You don't think we can pull this off, do you?"

"Well, pigs might fly." Ashimov lit a cigarette.

Dermot said, "Is it because of Dillon?"

Greta said, "Let's put it this way. I saw him in action in Iraq the other night, and if I hadn't seen it for myself, I wouldn't have believed it. So take care."

She and Ashimov went out, and Fahy exploded. "Dillon—fuggin' Sean Dillon. That's all we hear about." He reached for a raincoat. "I'm away out for a drink."

"And I'm with you," Regan told him. "What about you two?"

"We have things to do for our morning departure," Tod said. "But watch it, you two. Stay out of trouble."

They went out and Dermot put a large canvas bag on the table and opened it. He took out an AK-47 and passed it to Tod. "Give it a thorough check. I'll do the other."

"Pass me a silencer," which Dermot did. "What about

you? Do you really think we can pull this off?" Tod asked as he took the AK apart.

"We've done it before, we can do it again. We're still here, aren't we?"

"And so's Sean Dillon. That's the trouble."

A t about the same time, Belov landed at Ballykelly in the Republic, close to Drumore. Practically the first thing he did was phone Ashimov, who had just parked outside an Italian restaurant in Bayswater, Greta at his side.

"Bring me up to date," Belov demanded.

Ashimov did. "It's all in place."

"A lot of what-ifs," Belov said, "and I don't like that."

For once, Ashimov took the hard line. "No, I disagree. Kelly and Murphy have good reputations. Major Novikova's spadework has been excellent. This lead to Huntley Hall looks more than promising. I think we're in good shape."

"All right, I hear what you're saying. I'll stay here until we get some sort of resolution."

Greta said, "The great man?"

"Getting nervous. To hell with him. Let me buy you a nice dinner."

W alking along Wapping High Street, Fahy said to Regan, "This Dark Man pub the Salters own can't be far from here. Why don't we have a look?"

"Sounds good to me."

They made inquiries to a man at the newspaper stand on a corner, who directed them a couple of streets along to the left. They walked down between the old warehouses, came out on the wharf beside the Thames, and there was the Dark Man, a few cars parked nearby.

"The very place," Fahy said. "Shall we go in?"

"Let's take it slowly," Regan told him, and at that moment, lights approached down toward the wharf and they stepped back into shadows. A Range Rover stopped. Billy Salter got out and went into the pub.

"It's Salter," Fahy said. "Let's take a look."

They peered in through one of the windows. The bar was busy, but Billy was talking to Dillon at the counter.

Regan said, "Jesus, it's Dillon."

Fahy said, "Are you carrying?"

"No, mine's back in the weapon bag."

"So's mine. Christ. We could have taken a pop at him from the shadows."

"That's a fact," Regan said, although there was a certain relief in his voice.

"Well, there's one thing I can do." Fahy took out a switchblade knife and pushed the button. He jabbed it into the two front tires, which started to deflate. "That'll give Salter and bloody Dillon something to think about."

They were laughing like schoolboys as they cleared off. There was a final hiss of air from the tires and then an old and ravaged bag lady in layers of clothes, a woolen hat pulled over her head, stepped out of the darkness and took a look. She turned, put down her bags and went into the bar. She tapped Billy on the shoulder.

He turned. "Now then, Gladys, not in the bar."

"You'd better come outside, Billy, it's the big car of yours."

Billy frowned and Dillon swallowed his drink and went after him.

"The bastards," Billy said outside. "Who was it, Gladys?"

"Couple of men in raincoats. It is raining, Billy. One of them had one of those funny knives where the blade springs up, and he stuck it in the tires. They were laughing. They said, 'That will give Salter and bloody Dillon something to think about.'"

"Christ, if I get my hands on them." Billy kicked one of the tires.

"They were Irish," she said.

"Irish?" Billy said. "Bleeding Irish?"

"Hold it," Dillon told him. "You're sure, Gladys?"

"Oh, yes, they didn't speak like you. I mean, you're funny Irish. It was the other way."

"Who in the hell's got it in for me?" Billy said. "It doesn't make sense."

"Maybe it's something to do with me," Dillon said. "I know many Irishmen who could get very personal where I'm concerned. You'd better call the garage and see to the Range Rover. I've got to make a few inquiries. I'll see you later."

He hailed a cab on the High Street and told the driver to take him to Kilburn, where he started his rounds, working from pub to pub, talking to barmen, not that anything came up, but then it wouldn't. The IRA weren't operating in London. Those days had gone. And then, finally, there was the Green Man.

He went up the alley at the side, paused and peered in through the window. There he was, Danny Malone, a good comrade in the old days, but that was a long, long time ago. Danny was obviously going over his accounts, so Dillon tried the back door. It eased to his touch and he moved along the small hall, opened the door to the back room and went in.

Malone had been thinking about Dillon extremely uneasily since Kelly had mentioned him. In a sense, it had made him face up to what he was getting involved in, the kind of thing that had sent him to prison for fifteen years, and the fact that Dillon was involved made it worse. Now, he looked up and his face sagged.

"Sean, it's you."

"God save the good work, Danny," Dillon said and added, when Malone said nothing, "God save you kindly was the response to that. You're forgetting your manners."

"I'm sorry, Sean, I was so shocked. I mean, it's been years."

"Oh, I've had you in mind always, Danny."

Dillon lit a cigarette, and Malone's smile was ghastly. "So you work for Ferguson and the Prime Minister now."

"Oh, you know me, always the practical one. It got me out of a Serb prison. I was glad to hear they'd released you, Danny. Lucky for you the Peace Process came along when it did."

Malone was terrified, realizing just how stupid he'd been to get involved in the way he had, took a deep breath, and fought to keep control.

"Was there something you wanted, Sean?"

"Oh, just a word, Danny. My friend Billy Salter left his Range Rover outside the Dark Man at Wapping tonight. Two Irish guys came along, one of whom stuck a flick knife in two tires. They cleared off, laughing and saying it would give me and Billy something to think about."

Dillon reached under his coat, produced a Walther from his rear waistband, laid it on the table and lit another cigarette. "Any ideas, Danny, anyone in town from over the water?"

And Malone gave the performance of his life. "From over the water, Sean? You know yourself there's been nothing in London since the Peace Process. We all got early release. Take me. Fifteen years, but I only served five and the full sentence is still on the books. Any kind of involvement and I'm back inside to serve my full time. Do you think I'm mad? Who would be that crazy?"

Dillon said, "No, I suppose they'd have to be very stupid. I mean, what about that wife of yours, Jean? You wouldn't want to do anything to hurt her."

"She's hurting enough, Sean. Breast cancer."

"That's a damn shame," Dillon said, and meant it. He took a card from his pocket and dropped it on the table. "My mobile number is on there. Anything comes up, let me know."

He put the Walther back in his waistband and went out.

Malone went into the small toilet next door and was sick. He rinsed his face, then went back, found a bottle of whiskey and poured a large one. He was sweating and desperate to keep control. Boredom, a yearning for some action again, had made him respond to Kelly's phone call in the way he had. So foolish. Dillon had believed him, that was the important thing. But what to do about Kelly? If he left it, there was the chance that whatever the job was would fail anyway. On the other hand, it struck him that if he told Kelly of Dillon's appearance, it might be enough to make him abort the mission. He took a deep breath, picked up the phone and called Kelly at China Wharf.

And you're sure, absolutely sure, that Dillon bought your performance?"

"It would have got me work at the National Theatre. The business about my wife helped."

"Yes, that was a good ploy."

"Not a ploy, Dermot, true."

"Dammit, man, I'm sorry."

"It doesn't matter. What does is that I don't know what you're up to and I don't want to. On the other hand, the Dark Man is only a quarter of a mile away from China Wharf on the riverfront. If you want the two Irishmen who attended to Billy Salter's Range Rover, I think you know who they are, but it's your problem, not mine.

I'm out of the whole damn business. I've got a nice little villa in Spain where my wife is right now, resting in the sun, and I think I'll leave my bar staff in charge and go and join her."

He put the phone down, opened the office safe, found his passport, a checkbook and two thousand in mad money and phoned for a taxi to Heathrow. Then he ran upstairs and packed.

Fahy was first in through the door over at China Wharf, was tripped by Tod, went headfirst on his hands and knees, and received a severe kicking in the ribs from Kelly.

"Mind his face," Tod said, holding Regan still, an arm up his back.

At the appropriate moment, he released Regan and shoved him down to receive the same treatment. Finally, Tod heaved them to their feet and Kelly explained exactly what they'd done.

"Stupid, the pair of you, not a brain between you, and now I've lost Danny Malone." He slapped each one across the face. "You've got your orders, so stick to them. Do you understand me or do you want to go off the end of China Wharf into the Thames?"

They didn't have a word to say, he was a figure of such menace, and his ferocious reputation preceded him.

Tod said, "Go on, get out of it and go to bed." He turned to Kelly as they went out. "Are we still on?"

"Of course we are. There's no reason for Sean to suspect anything. Even Malone doesn't know why we're here, so tomorrow we'll go for a run in the country. Let's have a drink on it."

At Huntley Hall, the meal in the old oak-paneled room had been impressive by any standards. All of Selim's dietary requirements had been taken care of, although Ferguson had worked his way through roast beef and Yorkshire pudding with all the trimmings. Dalton and Miller acted as waiters, standing quiet and watchful, between the courses. Ferguson had drunk Burgundy, Selim mineral water.

Ferguson said, "Was the meal satisfactory?"

"Excellent."

"You can thank the Army Catering Corps."

"I'm impressed. There's not much sign of staff."

"Oh, they're there in their unobtrusive way. Let's go into the hall."

The hall was impressive, a floor of stone flags scattered with rugs, deep comfortable sofas, a log fire burning on a wide hearth. To one side, French windows with heavy curtains looked out over a terrace with a balustrade.

Selim sat in a wing-backed chair. "You do very well."

"Yes, it's a nice place." Ferguson turned to Miller. "I'll have a port if you don't mind, Staff Sergeant, a large one."

"Certainly, sir."

Miller went to a sideboard to get it and Ferguson sat opposite Selim. "I won't bother to offer you one."

"There was a time when I would have accepted with pleasure. In those days I didn't take my religion seriously. Public school, Cambridge and all that, and then, a few years ago, I changed."

"I can see how awkward that would have been for you."

"That I turned to Islam? Not at all. I'm British, General Ferguson, but also a Muslim. I have no difficulty with that. These islands have been home to an infinite variety of people since the Romans occupied them two thousand years ago."

"I suppose you're right. After all, I'm half Scots, half Irish." Ferguson finished his port and stood. "Let's have a breath of air on the terrace."

"That would be nice."

Dalton pressed a button and the French windows opened. Ferguson led the way outside. The air was fresh and damp, the shrubbery dense on the other side of the lawn, trees beyond. There were half a dozen garden statues out there, Roman figures revealed by security lights.

"We had a good start today," Ferguson said. "Our chat about Ashimov and Belov was very interesting."

"In a strange sort of way, Ashimov is angry with the world, and this manifests itself in his willingness to kill people. Belov simply wants to control the world. Power, ultimate power, is everything to him. He is someone to beware of much more than me, General."

"You're important enough. The list of organizations you've mentioned and the coded computer details of the young men that have been sent to Al Qa'eda training camps, that'll all be extremely helpful."

"May Allah forgive me."

It was then that Ferguson came to the important part. "You could be of enormous use to us, you know—not just now, but in the future."

"In betraying my own people?"

"What a shame," Ferguson said. "You've spoiled it. I thought you were British."

Selim groaned. "I didn't mean it that way. I'm speaking on behalf of my religion. I'm British, but a Muslim. In Tudor times, many people were Catholics at a time when this was forbidden, but still English. In fact, when some of them were trained for the priesthood in Rome . . ."

Ferguson broke in. "It was called the English College and they produced Jesuit priests known as 'Soldiers of Christ,' the best in the business."

"Many of whom died here in England for their faith."

"Well, let's try and see nothing like that happens to you," Ferguson said. "In we go. A decent night's sleep and we start again tomorrow."

The French windows closed behind them as they went inside. There was only the quiet and then an owl hooted, and there was a rustle in the shrubbery where a garden statue of some Roman emperor stood half revealed. Harold Laker peered out beside it, gazing toward the terrace at the scene inside the house through the French windows. He smiled, then disappeared back into the shrubbery and it was quiet again.

12

The following morning around ten, after breakfast, Kelly and Tod Murphy left in the Ford Transit and Fahy and Regan sat at the kitchen table, disgruntled, ribs aching.

"Now what?" Fahy asked.

"Don't ask me, Brendan," Regan replied.

"Maybe we should split up. I'll go and have a look at Roper's place, while you check out Dillon's cottage or the Bernstein woman's address."

"I thought Ashimov and Novikova were seeing to her?"

"Come off it. You're just trying to avoid anything to do with Dillon," Fahy said.

"That's a damn lie. Anything could happen. It's a sound idea to have a look at Bernstein, though."

"Okay, we'll use cabs," Fahy said. "We'll meet back

here in two or three hours. It's better than sitting round here like a gorilla in its own shit while Dermot and Tod go and have all the fun. I'm telling you, though, I'm not setting a foot out the door without a pistol in my pocket."

"Well, I'm with you there, so let's get on with it."

On the outskirts of Horsham, Kelly and Tod pulled in at a fuel station, filled up and went into the small café and ordered coffee.

Kelly lit a cigarette. "I wonder what those two idiots are getting up to. I don't trust them an inch. Maybe it wasn't such a good idea bringing them along."

"*Hmm.* Let me check," Tod said, and called Regan. "It's Tod. Where are you?"

"We're out and about. I'm checking Dillon's place and Fahy's having a look where Roper lives. I thought I might take in Bernstein's pad, too."

"Weren't you listening before? Ashimov and Novikova are on her case, so stay out of there. Familiarize yourself with Dillon's and Roper's places, but don't hang around, and don't try anything serious until you're told to."

"It's like talking to children," he said to Kelly after he'd clicked off.

"They've lost their edge," Kelly said. "Money in the pocket, too much booze and sitting around on their fat backsides at Drumore."

The mobile went and he answered. It was Ashimov. "Where are you?"

"Horsham. Quit worrying. We'll be there soon."

He rang off and said to Tod, "To hell with all of them. Let's you and me get on with it," and he led the way out.

Tod said as they walked to the Transit, "Why haven't you told him about Sean, and Danny Malone doing a runner?"

"Why bother the man? He might lose faith, and we can't have that." He unlocked the Transit. "Next stop, Huntley."

Greta Novikova left the Russian Embassy on foot from Kensington Palace Gardens, crossed to the pub on the other side and went in. Ashimov was seated at the bar reading a newspaper.

"Ah, there are you. Would you like a drink?"

"Not at the moment. What's going on?"

"I've spoken to Kelly. They were at Horsham."

"That's no more than half an hour to Huntley from there. Things ought to be happening soon."

"I hope so. But I've been around a long time, Greta. If it works, it works. If it doesn't, something else will come along. Survival is the name of the game."

"And you always do."

"Because I take precautions. For example, I have a company Falcon on standby at a flying club called Archbury about half an hour out of London. On standby until I tell it to stand down. Why? It's insurance. It means that if anything goes wrong, I can get the hell out of here quickly." He smiled. "I know, nothing will go wrong, you will say. And as a tribute to your faith, I intend to take you to lunch at the Ivy. Come on."

"But that's impossible to get into."

"The magic name of Belov works wonders, even at the Ivy." He had a hand on her elbow as they went out. "Let's go over to the embassy and pick up your Opel. I'll show you Bernstein's house on the way."

"That should be interesting. I've only seen a photo."

"A lady of some wealth, I'd say. You'll be surprised."

Regan had checked Stable Mews, but there was no sign of Dillon's Mini car outside the cottage. He didn't linger, but moved out to the square and hailed a cab. With a grin, he told the driver to take him to the end of Lord North Street, which was where Hannah Bernstein lived. When he got there, he walked a bit down the street toward Millbank and Victoria Tower Gardens and stood looking across.

In a way, he was just being bloody-minded, because he was angry at being put down by Tod as he had been. It was particularly unfortunate, given the circumstances, that Ashimov and Greta came down Lord North Street at that moment.

Ashimov, who was driving, said to her, "Impressed?" as they slowed at Hannah's house.

"Very," Greta told him. "I see what you mean."

They picked up speed, passing Regan on the corner, and she recognized him.

"My God, it's Regan, one of Kelly's men."

Ashimov pulled in at the curb. "Stupid bastard, he's not supposed to be here."

He got out of the Opel, Greta joined him and they advanced on Regan. "What in the hell are you doing here?" she demanded.

Regan, of course, recognized them instantly. "I was just having a look at the Bernstein woman's place."

"It's not your affair," she said. "You and your friend were told to check out Dillon's and Roper's places. We're seeing to Bernstein."

"All right," Regan told her. "I was just trying to get the job done. I've been to Dillon's."

"Just do as you're told," Ashimov advised him. "You understand me?"

"Okay, okay." Regan spread his hands. "No need to make a big case out of it." He turned, walked away and crossed through traffic to Victoria Tower Gardens, very angry indeed.

Ashimov drove away and was just as angry. "Peasants. Totally unreliable."

"You're right, they're clodhoppers," Greta said. "But, Yuri, the important thing is what's happening in Huntley. We can check on Bernstein later."

"And Dillon. I wonder what he's up to?"

"Never mind. Just get me to the Ivy. I'm starving."

At that moment, Dillon was entering the Piano Bar at the Dorchester Hotel, where he was warmly greeted by Guiliano, the manager.

"She's waiting for you," Guiliano said and led him to where Hannah Bernstein was sitting.

Hannah was looking terrific in a black Armani trouser suit. Dillon ordered two glasses of champagne, kissed her on the forehead and sat down.

"I've had a morning of paperwork," Dillon said. "It was intensely boring."

"Me, too. I didn't see you at the office."

"I did it at home. Any news?"

"Yes, Ferguson's phoned me twice. He's very pleased with the way things are going with Selim. Apparently, he had a real breakthrough and it's going well this morning."

"I had a minor development of a personal nature last night," and he told her what had happened to Billy Salter's Range Rover and his call on Danny Malone.

"There couldn't be any significance to it," she said. "We all know who Malone was. I helped put him away. He wouldn't do anything stupid enough to send him back to complete his sentence."

"I suppose even Danny couldn't be that silly. Anyway, a day of rest. Where do you want to have lunch? Mulligans?"

"No, right here will do for me, plus another glass of champagne."

"Sounds good to me," and he waved to Guiliano.

Regan, walking along by the Thames in a fury, rang Fahy. "Where are you?"

"Watching Roper. He left his house and went to a pub

on the corner of the main road. I checked the bar, and he was reading the paper in a booth by the window and the staff was making a big fuss over him. Ordered Irish stew."

"Well, he's got taste at least. I'm pissed off," and he told Fahy what had happened. "First of all, it's Tod kicking ass and then the bloody Russians."

"Oh, to hell with the lot of them. A decent meal and a glass, that's what you need."

"That's the first sensible thing I've heard all day. I could murder a pint. Where shall we go?"

And the reconnaissance turned to talk of pubs.

At Huntley, Kelly and Tod arrived to something of a surprise. Two of the trailers on the site behind the garage were occupied, cars parked outside, three children playing ball.

Kelly said, "Jesus Christ, that's just what we need."

"No, in fact that is exactly what we need. A couple of families around, kids playing." Tod shrugged. "A nice, normal environment." He got out of the Transit. "Come on, Dermot, do your stuff."

Betty Laker came out of the kiosk. "Fill it up?" she asked.

"No, actually," Dermot told her. "We're on our way from Brighton to London, and my nephew called in here—a big lad, in black leather, Suzuki motorcycle. Do you remember him?"

"Oh, I remember him," she said. Her grandfather came out of the kiosk behind her. She turned. "That young man on the motorcycle you were talking to in the pub. This gentleman is his uncle."

"Well, he met us in Brighton and told us what a nice place Huntley was. He mentioned the trailer site, so we thought we'd stop off and look around. Can you manage us?" Kelly asked.

"Of course we can," the old man said. "I'll handle this, Betty, love. Just follow me, gentlemen."

They parked by the other cars, the trailer was clean and decent, basically simple and perfectly acceptable. Tod, who was carrying two bags, dropped them on one of the beds.

"Looks fine to me."

"And what would you gentlemen be up to, then?" Laker asked, taking a cigarette from behind his ear and lighting it.

"Landscape gardening," Tod told him. "Mostly big estates. Places that have a problem, we get called in all over the country."

"You're Irish lads?"

"That's it," Kelly said. "Always on the go in our line of work. Never in one place more than a few weeks. It's hard graft."

"And it gives you an appetite," Tod intervened. "There's a pub around here, I believe."

"There certainly is, and the food's good. I'll show you the way."

Tod opened one of the bags and there was a clunk as he took out two bottles of Scotch and put them on the side. The old man licked his lips.

"You're well supplied, I'll give you that."

"I don't like to run out, and that's a fact." Kelly smiled. "But let's go over to the pub now and get something to eat. Maybe you'd join us?"

"Be glad to," Laker said and led the way out.

The three of them had shepherd's pie, the Scotch whiskey flowed and the old man loved it.

Tod said, "Funny place this. Dermot's nephew was telling us about the big house."

"Huntley Hall? I know all about that."

"Yes, so he told us."

"And what he knew was what he'd heard from you," Kelly said. "He passed it on the way in. Huntley Hall Institution. They've certainly got some security there. I mean, some of the big country estates we've worked on have got walls like that, but that electronic fence on top is something else again."

Tod slipped off to the bar and got three more large whiskeys. He brought them back and pushed one over to Laker, who took it with alacrity.

"Ah, it's special, see. They have to have that kind of security, cameras and so forth, to keep people in. They're all head cases, that's the story. It's not like it was in Lord Faversham's day. I was telling your nephew, a poacher's paradise that estate were."

Tod eased another whiskey over to him. "Not any longer. Not if there's no way of getting in now. You certainly can't climb that fence!"

"Oh, I don't know. There's ways and there's ways. You don't always need to go over a fence."

"You've got a point there," Tod said. "You could go under, I suppose."

"Now, I never said that, never did," Laker said, and accepted another whiskey that was pushed his way.

"No, I don't believe it," Kelly said. "There's no way you could get in a place like that."

"Well, I wouldn't be too sure." Laker was already drunk and a little belligerent.

Tod said, "It doesn't sound likely to me, I admit. In fact, I'd bet on it."

The hook was there, and Laker took it. "You put your money where your mouth is and I'll bloody well show you."

"All right." Kelly took out his wallet and produced two fifty-pound notes. "There you go. A hundred quid says you're making it up."

Laker's eyes gleamed and he reached for the money, but Kelly snatched his hand away. "Oh, no, you prove me wrong if you want this."

"I bloody well will." Laker reached for the remaining whiskey and swallowed it down. He got up. "Come on, then. I'll show you whether I'm lying or not," and he made for the door.

He led the way along the road out of the village, no more than five minutes' walk, then turned into a track leading through heavy woodland. It was very quiet, only the birds making noise, lifting off and calling to each other.

In spite of the drink taken, Laker was surprisingly steady on his feet. "This is Witch Wood. Don't ask me why, but so it's been called that since time long gone. If you could see through the trees, maybe fifty yards to the left is the main road, and the Huntley Hall estate on the other side."

"So what are we talking about here?" Tod asked as they walked along the track.

"Round about eighteen hundred, Lord Ashley Faversham made a fortune in the sugar trade in Barbados, then came home to refurbish the family estate. But there was a problem. There used to be a river on the far side of the woods and it would overflow. It doesn't exist now. It was diverted a long time ago to provide water for a canal project. But when it was there, and there was water seepage into the estate, Faversham had a series of tunnels built to run it off."

"And?"

"And when the river was diverted, they had the tunnels closed off."

Tod could already see the way this was going. He took out his cigarettes and gave Laker one. "Except one of them was overlooked, wasn't it?"

Lake almost choked on his cigarette. "How did you know that?"

"Oh, I've got that kind of mind," Tod said. "Just show me where it is."

They plowed on, and Kelly said, "How long have you known about this?"

"Since I were a lad," Laker said. "My dad told me. It were a secret in the family, and still is."

"Good man, yourself," Tod said. "Now let's be seeing it."

A few minutes later, Laker turned left off the track, pushed into a thicket, paused, bent down, fumbled in the grass, found a handle and lifted an iron grille. The hole was quite wide. "I'll lead the way," he said, and started down an iron ladder.

Below, it was damp, no more than that, with headroom to five feet. As Tod followed him, Kelly behind, Laker took a flashlight from his pocket. "Follow me."

He took off, and after a while, rays of light drifted through from above. "Airholes," he said. "That means we're under the road and into the gardens."

A few minutes later, they came to the end and another iron ladder gave way to another iron grille. He mounted first and pushed the grille back, and they followed and found themselves in a copse of dense foliage. The house was clearly visible through the trees.

"You've got security lighting mounted on the house over the terrace. There's a camera on the left and another on the right. More stuff like that on the drive. The real problem is the wall. Even if you got over it, there's an electronic beam five foot inside. It *should* take care of anything."

"Except for a tunnel that they never knew about," Tod said.

"Exactly."

They moved forward, paused behind a couple of statues and looked across at the terrace. Just then, the French windows opened and Selim walked out, Ferguson behind him.

Kelly said, "Christ, it's them."

At the same moment, it started to rain and Laker said, "Right, let's get out of here," and he turned and started back to the access grille to the tunnel.

Kelly grabbed at Tod's arm as they went after him. "You saw who that was?"

"Of course I did."

"Christ, Tod, if we'd had a gun between us, it would have been so simple. Not only Selim, but Ferguson as well."

"And simple is what it will be," Tod said. "We'll be back, Kelly, ould son, never you fear," and they went after the old man.

When they surfaced at the entrance, Laker was in high spirits. "Did I tell you or did I tell you?" he chorused as they went back through Witch Wood. "That's a hundred quid for me."

"You're right, old son," Kelly told him. "I was wrong and you were right. I wouldn't have believed it if I hadn't seen it for myself."

They reached the trailer site, and Tod said, "You owe the man a hundred quid, Dermot, so get it out and we'll have a drink on it."

He led the way into their trailer, got one of the bottles

of Scotch open and found three glasses. Kelly gave the old man the two fifty-pound notes and Tod handed him the glass of Scotch.

"Bottoms up, me ould son, you deserve it."

Laker was thoroughly drunk now, and took the whiskey down in a long swallow. "Yes, I bloody well do."

Tod gave him the bottle. "Go on, you've earned it. Get off and have a lie down and we'll see you later."

The old man clasped the bottle to his chest, lurched out of the door and staggered off toward the bungalow at the back of the garage.

"Now, there's a happy man," Kelly said and closed the door against the driving rain. "So, what do you think?"

"That we go back later in the day," Tod said. "And we see if we get lucky. Only this time, we'll be armed."

Kelly grinned. "You know, I'm actually believing it's going to work. I'm even believing we could call Smith up and have him back over here tonight."

"And where would that leave Fahy and Regan?"

"We could give them a call, tell them to walk away from the London end of things, get a plane to Dublin." Kelly grabbed Tod by his arm. "For God's sake, Tod, Ashimov wanted Selim and he gets him with Ferguson. To hell with the others, even Dillon. You can't do much better than that."

"You've got a point, Dermot, but let's see. We've still got to think of Regan and Fahy."

"Fuck them," Kelly said. "If they can't see to themselves, that's their problem. Now let's have another drink on it and decide when we're going back in."

After a lunch that had contained considerably more than a single glass, Regan and Fahy wandered the streets for a while. Finally, rain coming down, Regan said to Fahy, "What now? Back to China Wharf?"

"To hell with that," Fahy said. "Let's try the Roper fella's place again. I'm tired of just standing around doing nothing. Something might turn up."

"I'm with you. Do we ring Dermot and Tod first?"

"All we'll get is a bollocking again."

"Then let's just go," and Regan stepped to the pavement and hailed a cab.

In Regency Square, Roper had been looking at computer screens too long and was opening his mouth for a yawn when his mobile rang.

"It's Sean. What's up?"

"I'm tired, stressed, and I've been sitting at this damn thing too long. I need a break," Roper said.

"How about I come round and take you out for a drink or something?"

"Sounds good to me."

Roper felt better already and reached in his pocket for cigarettes and found the pack was empty. He cursed. He'd been kept alive from his terrible injuries by a cocktail of drugs, and tobacco had become a mainstay. It was the same for a lot of soldiers in his situation, and the need was overpowering. He'd have to go out to the corner shop.

He made for the front door, got it open and found it was raining. He took an umbrella from the hall stand, pressed one of the electronic buttons on his wheelchair to close the door behind him, went down the ramp to the pavement and raised the umbrella. He sailed, in a way, down the pavement, strangely exhilarated, down to the shop on the corner, where Mr. Khan had installed a ramp at one of the doors especially to facilitate Roper's comings and goings.

A large, bearded Muslim with a genial smile and a Cockney accent, Khan greeted Roper warmly. "What you run out of now, Major?"

"Cigarettes," Roper said. "The old cancer sticks. I'll take a carton of the usual."

"Maybe you should try and give up," Khan said, as he got the carton and took Roper's money.

"And live longer, you mean, in my state?" Roper stowed the carton in a side pocket of the wheelchair. "Wouldn't make much difference."

Khan tried to keep smiling, because he liked Roper. "Now then, Major, it's not like you to be gloomy."

"You're right. I'll be Cheerful Charlie from now on."

He turned his wheelchair, and Khan said, "There was a man in here this morning asking if I knew where you lived."

"Oh, yes?"

"An Irish geezer, Ulster I'd say, you know what I mean? It's a different kind of Irish accent, isn't it?"

And Roper, veteran of the Irish troubles for twenty years, the finest bomb-disposal man in the business, stopped smiling. "It certainly is. What did he want?"

"Didn't say. Just asked if I knew you. The thing is, I saw him again with another guy a little while ago, and he sounded the same as they walked past."

"Thanks," Roper said. "I'll keep an eye out."

He moved onto the pavement, put up his umbrella and took a Codex Four from his pocket and called Dillon.

"Where are you?"

"In a cab on my way. Traffic's lousy."

"The fact is, I could have a problem. My friendly local shopkeeper, Mr. Khan, you know him, tells me I've been inquired about."

"And by whom would that be?" Dillon asked.

"Couple of men, Northern Irish accents. I've got a lot of history there, Sean."

"Where are you now?"

"On the street, on my way home."

"Take it easy, just get inside. I'll be there in ten minutes. Are you carrying?"

"Of course."

"Good man."

He switched off, and Roper started along the pavement.

Regan and Fahy, standing in a doorway on the other side of the road, sheltering from the rain, saw him approach.

"The man himself," Fahy said.

"What do we do?" Regan already had his hand on the butt of a Browning in his raincoat pocket.

"Wait," Fahy said. "Not out here on the street. Let him

get himself together, then we move very fast over the road and help him inside."

Roper did his usual maneuver, turned to position, opened the door electronically, then started up the ramp. Quickly, Regan and Fahy darted over the road, and Fahy grabbed the end of the wheelchair.

"Let's help you, Major," he said and pushed Roper in. Regan followed them and closed the street door behind them.

"Now then, Major, let's talk," Fahy said, and pushed Roper into the living room beside his computer banks.

Roper sat there facing them, no fear in him at all. Regan said, "Do we call Dermot and Tod, Brendan?"

"Don't be stupid, Fergus," Fahy said. "You'll be wanting to call Ashimov next. This is our affair."

"Dermot and Tod? That would be as in Kelly and Murphy," Roper said. "Which means that you two idiots are Regan and Fahy."

"And how would you be knowing that?" Regan demanded.

"Because you're thick and stupid. You think we don't know all about you? You work for Ashimov, and that means you work for Josef Belov. Where's Belov now? Drumore Place? Does he know you're here?"

"You think you're clever, don't you?" Fahy said. "Too clever for your own good. We'll have to do something about that," and he took the Browning from his pocket.

13

At that precise moment in time, Kelly and Tod were moving through Witch Wood and paused at the iron grille in the thicket. They both wore hooded anoraks against the rain. Dermot had phoned Smith from the trailer, had told him to do the return flight to Dunkley at once. Smith had been unable to conceal his reluctance, but had soon seen the error of his ways.

Kelly and Tod lit cigarettes. "Well, this is it," Tod said. "This is where the luck comes in."

"Oh, you always need that."

"What about Fahy and Regan, or Ashimov, for that matter?" Tod asked.

"Later," Kelly said, "when we've got the good news. Now let's get it done."

He pulled up the iron grille, went down the ladder and Tod dropped the weapon bag down and went after him.

A short while later, at the end of the tunnel, they paused and opened the weapons bag. Tod produced an AK and a silencer and passed them to Kelly, took out another for himself. Kelly went up the ladder, opened the grille and exited, and Tod followed him. They moved through the dense foliage of the copse and crouched behind the Roman statues. It was quiet, only the occasional bird calling, and the rain hissed down steadily.

"Come on," Kelly said. "Make my day."

"That was a movie," Tod murmured. "This could take more patience, so *be* patient."

In the sitting room, Ferguson and Selim were having tea at the end of an exhausting session. Dalton and Miller stood watchful as usual, as the two men talked.

"Open the French windows, Staff Sergeant," Ferguson said to Dalton. "Let's have a breath of air."

"Certainly, sir."

Dalton pressed the button and the windows opened. "I like it," Selim said. "The smell of the rain in the countryside, the sound of it falling through the trees."

"I know what you mean," Ferguson said, and hesitated. "You know, Doctor, you obviously have a genuine love of your native land. Do you regret having been born in London?"

"No, I love the damn place." He laughed as he got to his feet. "I'm remembering something Mr. Dillon said to me. That I should remember there are mosques all over London."

He moved to the open windows, and Ferguson joined him. "Then what were you thinking of?"

"There is a passage in the Koran, General, that says one sword is worth ten thousand words. Perhaps that is what I was thinking of."

And at that moment, Kelly shot him between the eyes, fragmenting the back of his skull. As the body hurtled back, bouncing against Ferguson, the General leaned over slightly to catch it and Tod Murphy's bullet went askew, slicing Ferguson across the left shoulder. He sank to the floor, clutching Selim, and Dalton and Miller darted past, each drawing a Beretta and firing blindly into the woods, but Kelly and Tod were already working their way back through the copse and dropping down through the grille.

"I got him," Kelly said. "Clear in my sight, right between the eyes."

They stowed the rifles in the bag and hurried along the tunnel. "Not Ferguson," Tod said. "I hit him, that's a fact, but he moved at the last minute. I think I clipped his shoulder."

"Never mind, it's a grand day's work, that's the truth of it," Kelly said. "Come on, let's get out of here and make for Dunkley and that Navajo. We've made our bonus for our Russian friends on this one. Belov will pay us in gold bars."

They were back at the village in fifteen minutes, put their belongings together and stowed them in the Transit. Tod went to the kiosk by the fuel pumps and found Betty.

He got his wallet out. "I've just had a phone call. We're needed in London, like yesterday."

"That's a shame," she said.

"What do I owe you?"

She told him, and he paid her. "It's a smashing place, and we'll be back."

He jumped in the Transit, got behind the wheel and drove away. Kelly was on a high, produced a bottle of whiskey and swallowed. "Jesus, but we did it." He got his mobile out. "I'll ring Fahy, tell him that he and Regan should move it."

He tapped out the number, and when it connected, said, "It's Dermot, Brendan."

"And it's Dillon here, you bastard, what do you think about that?"

At Roper's place, after Fahy had drawn the Browning from his pocket, things had not gone as he and Regan had expected. Roper hadn't seemed to care, had stayed incredibly calm.

"What do I get, summary execution, IRA-style? You gentlemen have tried to shoot me and blow me up many times, and I'm still here. I need a smoke."

He took the carton of Marlboros from the side pocket of his wheelchair, pulled a pack out and extracted a cigarette. "Anyone got a light?" he asked, as he replaced the pack in the side pocket, only this time when his hand came out, it clutched a Walther, which he jammed against Fahy's knee and pulled the trigger. Fahy cried out and fell back, dropping his Browning.

At the same moment, Dillon's voice echoed over the voice box. "Roper, it's me."

Regan, confused, stood over Fahy, who was being noisy.

Roper called, "They're here, Sean, one down, one to get." He pressed the electronic door button and raised his Walther to Regan, who ducked out into the corridor and ran for the rear of the house.

Dillon burst in, gun in hand, and found Fahy groaning, Roper leaning over him. "There was Regan, Sean, and he cleared off through the kitchen."

"Call Rosedene," Dillon said. "Get the paramedics in. I'll be back."

He got to the front door and saw Regan hurrying down the pavement. Regan glanced over his shoulder and started to run. Dillon went after him, past the corner shop. Regan kept running headlong, scattering a few people on the pavement, then lurched into the main road as a red London double-decker bus came along and bounced him into the air.

Traffic came to a halt, and people milled around as the driver got out of the bus. A police car turned out of the traffic stream and eased beside the bus. Dillon paused and listened, saw one of the policemen drop to one knee and examine Regan. He shook his head.

"He's dead."

The driver was shocked. "It wasn't my fault."

More than one person called out, "That's right. He ran into the road, head down."

Dillon turned discreetly and walked away.

When he rejoined Roper, he found him holding the Walther on Fahy, who was clutching his trousered knee with both hands, groaning. Dillon went into the kitchen, found a couple of towels, went back, knelt and tied them tightly around Fahy's knee.

"You always were a stupid bastard, Brendan, so stop moaning and listen. We use a private clinic called Rosedene. They're on their way, so you won't bleed to death. However, this isn't a public hospital. It's high security, so you belong to Ferguson now. Understand?"

"Yes," Fahy moaned.

"Play ball and you could stay out of prison. You understand that, too?"

"Yes."

"So tell me the whole story, and make it quick or I might put one in the other knee."

And talk Fahy did. It was just as he finished that the mobile in his pocket sounded.

It's Dermot, Brendan."

"And it's Dillon here, you bastard, what do you

think about that? Regan's dead and Fahy's in a poor way. He's spilled his guts, too. I know everything."

"Like hell you do," Kelly said wildly. "We got Selim and Ferguson. I bet you don't know *that*. It was a good payday, Sean. Go to hell."

He switched off and said to Tod, "Put your foot down."

Tod did as he was told. "What's happened?"

Kelly told him.

Tod said, "What now?"

"We get to Dunkley and move the hell out of here."

"As long as Smith's there."

"He'll be there," Kelly said grimly. "He wouldn't dare not to be."

"You'd better let Ashimov know."

"I suppose so. I'd like to leave him to rot in hell, but there's Belov to consider. He's got a long arm, that one."

After a lengthy afternoon at the Ivy, Ashimov and Greta had called in at the Old Red Lion in Farley Street and were sitting in a booth by the fire when his phone sounded. They'd been laughing over a shared joke, and he was still laughing when he put the phone to his ear.

"Ashimov."

As he listened, the smile vanished and his face was terrible to see. "So that's it? You're not even sure about Ferguson? And Fahy's spilling his guts to Dillon?"

"Jesus, man, we got Selim for you. He was the main priority, and Ferguson's damaged, I swear."

"And now you're running for it?"

"Flying for it, and if you've got any sense, you'll do the same. We'll see you at Drumore."

"Oh, you'll see me at Drumore, all right."

"Don't get smart with me, Ashimov. Drumore is my patch. You need me and you need my friends. Since the Peace Process, the Brits haven't been able to lay a finger on us in the Irish Republic. You'd do well to remember that. You need us!"

He rang off, and Greta demanded, "For God's sake, what is it?"

He explained. When he was finished, she said, "It could be bad, right?"

"Could be? How the hell do you think Belov's going to take it? Especially after what Fahy's no doubt blurted out to Dillon? My career, my association with Belov, are on the line." He punched a number into his phone. "Archbury? Connect me with Captain Kelso."

"You're going?" she said.

"I think it would be the smart thing if we both went." Kelso's voice came on. "It's me," Ashimov told him. "I've got Major Novikova with me. We should be with you in forty-five minutes. Immediate takeoff, destination Ballykelly."

"What about Belov?" she said. "We'd best get it over with."

"I suppose so." He called Belov at the castle on his private mobile and was answered at once.

"Yuri, I've been waiting. How are things?"

"Good news and bad news."

He went over events very briefly. There was a long pause, and Belov switched off without a word.

The rage in Ashimov was obvious. "Ferguson's people, his whole enterprise, have been nothing but trouble ever since Manhattan, and this Dillon has been a stone in my shoe. It's all gone down the toilet, the years of kowtowing to Belov, doing his dirty work. He doesn't make allowances, Greta, it's how he is." He rose, took her arm roughly. "Come on, let's get moving."

"To the embassy?"

"No way. Straight to Archbury. I'm taking no chances. I'm not even calling in at my place."

At Huntley Hall, the duty medical officer had done his best with Ferguson's left shoulder. The bullet had plowed through close to the edge.

"It's Rosedene for you, General," the young Medical Corps captain said. "It's a decent patching job I've done, but you could do with a scan, and Professor Henry Bellamy is far better at embroidery than I am. You're going to need some good work. AK rounds really leave a mark."

"And you would know, Wilson?"

"Six months in Iraq, sir. The second injection I've given will hold you to London, but don't disturb the sling. Let me help you with your jacket."

Which he did, and Ferguson said, "And Dr. Selim?"

"Bagged and awaiting the disposal unit, General."

"Let's get him to the North London crematorium. The latest incinerators don't take much more than an hour, and all that's left is six pounds of gray ash. Do you mind your work for my department after Iraq, all the Official Secrets stuff?"

"Good God, no, sir, it's infinitely more interesting."

"As long as you can accept the importance of what we do. We're at war, too, you see, Captain."

He walked out into the hall and found Dalton and Miller. Dalton said, "The disposal team just collected Dr. Selim, General."

"Good, then we can get back to London."

In the back of the Land Rover, he called Dillon, who had driven back to Roper's place in his Mini car. They'd spoken earlier when Dillon had phoned Huntley Hall in a panic after Kelly's claim to have gotten Ferguson as well as Selim. The General had just been about to undergo treatment in surgery, so not much information had been exchanged.

"Just tell me everything, Sean, so I get the full picture." Which Dillon did, and Ferguson said, "My goodness, Ashimov's got plenty to answer for."

"All done on Belov's behalf with Belov's power and money behind him, and Roper's hunch is that Belov's at Drumore."

"An interesting pattern. He not only wanted Selim shut up for good, but the rest of us—me, you, Major Roper. Even the Salters."

"Well, we did spoil the plot to assassinate President Cazalet, and then there was Baghdad. With a few other things that happened, I guess we screwed up things big-time for Belov."

"I suppose the only person who seems to have avoided his wrath is Superintendent Bernstein. You've told her what's happened?"

"Haven't been able to. Both Roper and I have been try-ing, but there's been no response on her mobile phone."

"What on earth's going on?"

"It's all right, General. I got through to her grandfa-ther, who told me she'd gone to the wedding of an old friend in Windsor this afternoon. That's what people do at weddings, they switch off."

"Well, keep trying. Ashimov's still out there some-place."

At Dunkley, there was rain and fog and things were down and Smith was sweating, taking the biggest chance of his life. At any other time, he would have aborted, but he knew what Kelly's people might do to him back home if he failed.

In the Transit at the side of the airstrip, Kelly and Tod waited, listening to the sound of the Navajo as Smith made one pass and then two.

"The bastard," Kelly said, as the sound faded again. "He's doing a runner."

"Give him a chance, Dermot. This weather is bad news. Maybe you'd like him to crash?"

There was the sound of the engines again, and at the

controls, Smith went lower and lower, despairing at the gray cotton wool that seemed to surround him, and then suddenly, at four hundred feet, the runway appeared and he bounced down. It was one of the worst landings of his career, but he'd made it. He taxied to the far end, turned, and Tod drove toward him in the Transit. He and Kelly jumped out and Smith left the cockpit and opened the Airstair door. Kelly led the way in.

"You fuck, what were you trying to do, frighten us?"

After him, Tod helped Smith wrestle with the door. He put a hand on Smith's shoulders. "You did well."

"I just took ten years off my life, Tod, never again. I've had it, I mean it. You can keep your money in future."

He was into the cockpit and back to work, the plane hurtling along the runway and rising into the fog, as Tod sat across from Kelly and fastened his seat belt. Kelly had a bottle of whiskey out and swallowed from it.

He laughed wildly. "We did it. We did it, and we got away with it."

"Actually, it's Smith who's gotten us away with it."

"He's being paid, isn't he?" He offered the whiskey bottle. "Have a drink."

"I don't think so." Tod lit a cigarette. "I need my head clear for Drumore. For little things like Belov and Ashimov."

"I can handle them, Tod. I can handle Ashimov. We've survived worse things than those two. They need us more than we need them." He raised the bottle. "Up the IRA."

"Yes, right up," Tod said.

Hannah had caught a commuter train from Windsor to London after the wedding reception. It was early evening, dusk falling, when she came out of King's Cross Station and found an enormous taxi line. She hesitated, debating whether to wait it out, then decided on the bus instead and walked to the main road. She was sitting on the top deck looking out when her mobile went. It was Dillon.

"Jesus, woman, I've been trying to get you for hours."

"I've been to a wedding."

"Yes, while you've been having fun and sipping champagne, the roof's fallen in. Listen."

When he was finished explaining, she was horrified. "So what's happening now?"

"Selim is on his way to oblivion, and Ferguson to Rosedene, where he's going to need some attention from Henry Bellamy. Kelly and Tod Murphy? If I know the score, I'd say they've flown straight back to Louth from this Dunkley place."

"And Ashimov?"

"Roper says that a Belov International Falcon landed at Ballykelly yesterday and it's still there. That means Belov must be at Drumore Place. But Ashimov is still a loose cannon. Where are you?"

"On top of a number-nine bus on my way home."

"Listen, Hannah, this guy has made it personal. He wants the whole team, even the Salters, and we don't know where he is. You go straight home. I'm coming to get you. Now, watch yourself."

Ashimov had taken the wheel of Greta's Opel and drove recklessly now through the traffic, to Greta's alarm.

"Watch it, Yuri, for God's sake."

He was simmering with rage. "I've been watching it all my life and I'm still here." That terrible scar on his face seemed to stand out. "I'm the original survivor, never forget that," and he swerved around a truck and plowed on.

Hannah got off the bus at Millbank and started toward Victoria Tower Gardens. She paused at the curb, allowing the traffic to pass, then started across to Lord North Street. Ashimov recognized her at once as she crossed the road in front of him.

"It's the Bernstein bitch," and he dropped a gear, swung across the road and went after her.

She turned into Lord North Street and saw Dillon's Mini car outside her house and he was standing at the door. She called and waved and hurried toward him as Ashimov swerved behind her.

Dillon had turned, was plainly identifiable, and Ashimov said, "I'll get them, I'll get both of them."

And as they closed on Hannah, Dillon saw them, recognized them, and his mouth opened in a cry of warning. Hannah half turned, but there was no time. Ashimov crowded her on the pavement, bouncing her to one side, and Dillon drew his Walther and fired, but the Opel swerved, his bullet passing through the roof as it hurtled past.

"For God's sake, Yuri," Greta Novikova said.

"Just shut up," he said, "and let's get to that damned airport," and he put his foot down.

On the pavement, Hannah Bernstein was trying to haul herself up, clutching at the railings as Dillon got to her. "You're all right, just hold on to me." But there was blood coming down her face, and he was afraid.

She spoke, but as from a distance. "It was Ashimov, Sean, and the woman."

"I know, look, just do as I say." He eased her around to the passenger seat, got behind the wheel, took out his mobile and phoned Roper and explained what had happened as he started the car. "Phone Rosedene. Tell them I'm on my way and we're going to need Bellamy."

"Leave it to me."

Dillon drove away, Hannah leaning back, moaning. Strange, he didn't feel some hot burning rage. If anything, he was cold and conscious of only one thing: Ashimov was responsible for this.

LONDON

IRELAND

14

At Rosedene, Dillon paced nervously up and down in reception, smoking cigarette after cigarette. Rabbi Julian Bernstein sat by the window.

"Sean, sit down. It isn't helping and it isn't good for you."

"If anything goes wrong with her"—Dillon had that Devil's face on him—"I swear I'll . . ."

"You'll do nothing. We wait, we see. 'Vengeance is mine' achieves nothing."

"What do I do, turn the other cheek? Well, I'm feeling very Old Testament right now."

His mobile sounded. It was Roper. "How is she?"

"I'm waiting to hear. What have you got?"

"I've tracked down another Belov plane which lifted

off half an hour ago from Archbury. Ashimov and Novi-kova are aboard."

"Dammit," Dillon told him. "That really rubs it in. That she's gone with him, I mean."

"There's something else you won't like. The Opel car. It's a Russian Embassy vehicle logged out to a Novikova."

"Well, there you are," Dillon said. "Make my day. What's the intended destination of the plane?"

"Ballykelly. Belov International's got a big develop-ment there, which includes an airstrip. Belov dropped in yesterday, which means he's already at Drumore Castle."

"Surprise, surprise," Dillon said.

"Safely in the Republic of Ireland, where they can't be touched."

"Not if I can help it."

"Well, you'll have to hurry, Sean. Air Traffic Control in Dublin reports a slot booked out at ten o'clock tomor-row morning for Belov's Falcon to Moscow."

At that moment, the door opened and Ferguson came in, supported by Miller and Dalton. His face was gray, eyes sunken. They helped him to a chair.

He looked at Dalton. "Be a good chap. Find us some whiskey. They'll have some in the back for medicinal purposes."

Dalton went away, and Dillon said, "You look terrible."

"Yes, well, being shot does have that effect. But never mind me. How is the Superintendent?"

"Bellamy's with her now. They did a scan."

Ferguson turned to Rabbi Bernstein. "This life of Hannah's, Rabbi, you must hate it, all of it."

The old man smiled gently. "It's the life she chose, General. It's what she wanted. And you do look awful. My son is at a medical conference in Paris, but I've phoned him and he's coming back at once. No," he said, as Ferguson started to protest, "I insist. He'd never forgive himself otherwise. And I wouldn't forgive myself, either."

At Doone, the Navajo had landed. Smith taxied up to the hangar and switched off. He got the Airstair door open and Kelly and Tod followed him out. Kelly clapped him on the shoulder.

"You did a good job, I'm proud of you. Tod will take care of you."

"I don't want anything. Just leave me alone. Never again." Smith closed the Airstair door.

Kelly said, "You never say that to me. I call, you jump."

"Go on, then, put a bullet in my head now." Smith shook his head. "As far as I'm concerned, the IRA can go to hell. You're stuck in the past anyway."

Kelly grabbed at him, but Tod pulled him back. "Just let it go. We'll go down to the Royal George and have a drink with the boys."

At Ballykelly as the Falcon touched down, it was quiet in the cabin. Ashimov had drunk steadily, and barely exchanged a word with Greta. They rolled to a halt. Kelso switched off and Brown left the cockpit and opened the door. As they stepped down, a Land Rover approached.

"Well, here we go," Ashimov said. "To an uncertain future." He hesitated. "You're with me in this, Greta?"

"Of course I am," and yet, in her heart, she didn't know what that meant.

"Then let's get on with it. Beard the ogre in his den."

They went down the steps, and to Ashimov's astonishment, Josef Belov got out from behind the wheel of the Land Rover.

"So there you are. I've been waiting."

Professor Henry Bellamy came in, stripping off his gloves, and paused in front of Ferguson.

"For God's sake, Charles, at your age you can't afford this kind of thing."

Dalton held out a file. "Captain Wilson sent this, sir."

"Never mind me," Ferguson said. "What about Hannah?"

"She has a broken collarbone and right arm, and a depressed fracture of the skull." He turned to Bernstein. "I'm sorry, Rabbi, but I'm transferring her to the neurological unit at the Cromwell. I've called in George Dawson, he's the best in the business."

"How bad is it?" Bernstein asked. "What are her chances?"

"Oh, excellent. Dawson is world-class. But I should point out one thing."

"And what's that?"

Bellamy glanced at Ferguson. "The other year when that Party of God hit man tried to kill her, she suffered damage to the stomach, a bullet to the left lung and a chipped spine. It was a miracle she survived."

"Thanks to a great surgeon," Dillon said.

"Which means nothing, Sean. She'll survive this, too, don't worry, but her future will be more problematic. This may well be the end of her career."

"But it means everything to her," Dillon said.

"I know. Maybe she could have a desk job. I don't know—but there are limits to the endurance of the human body."

"Of course, "Bernstein said.

"An ambulance is picking her up at any moment, which will take her to Dawson at the Cromwell. You, of course, may go with her, Rabbi."

"Thank you."

Bellamy opened Wilson's file, had a quick look and shook his head. "Straight in, Charles, this is far worse than I'd expected." He turned to Dalton and Miller. "Take him through."

They got Ferguson up between them. He glanced at Dillon. "Don't do anything stupid, Sean."

"Now, would I do anything like that?" Yet the eyes burned in his face and there was that look of the Devil about him again.

Ferguson said, "You're going to go after him."

"You can depend on it."

"And nothing I say to dissuade you would work?"

"Not this time."

Ferguson said, "Then all our departmental resources are available to you. Just be careful, Sean." He smiled wearily, and Dalton and Miller took him out between them, Bellamy following.

The Rabbi said, "I've seen that look on your face before. Maybe she wouldn't want it."

"Ashimov did it deliberately. I witnessed it myself. He pays in full."

"God help you, Sean."

An ambulance driver looked in. "Rabbi Bernstein?"

"That's me." The old man glanced at Dillon, sighed and went out.

It was quiet in reception, and Dillon took a deep breath and lit a cigarette, then he phoned Roper.

"How is she?"

Dillon explained and added, "Ferguson's in a poor way himself. Bellamy's just taken him into the operating room. Before that, though, the old boy gave me the use of all our departmental resources."

"Does this mean what I think it does?"

"Absolutely. Will you stay on the line, make sure there aren't any changes in departure plans at Ballykelly?"

"Sean, you're crazy. You'll never get away with it. It's as if you've got a death wish."

"I'll ring Lacey and arrange a drop. The beach at Drumore will do nicely, but you check the weather and confirm it with him. Speak to the Quartermaster for me and arrange some weaponry."

"I'll get on it. But you can't do this on your own, not even the great Sean Dillon."

"Oh, I won't." Dillon went out, got in the Mini and

phoned Farley Field. "It's Dillon. I need Squadron Leader Lacey."

He droned on through traffic one-handed and Lacey came on. "Sean?"

"Nothing has ever been more important, so don't argue. Ferguson's been shot, he's in a hospital operating room at the moment, and he's charged me with full authority. I'll be with you in perhaps an hour. You're going to fly in over Drumore in County Louth and do a beach drop."

"I'm not sure about the weather, Sean."

"We've done it before in worse. This one is important. We take it right to the edge."

"As you say, Sean."

He switched off, and Dillon carried on. One more place to call.

When he entered the Dark Man, Harry Salter, Billy, Joe Baxter and Sam Hall were in the end booth having a drink, except for Billy and his usual orange juice.

Harry said, "So here you are. You're hardly keeping us up-to-date."

"Just shut up and listen," Dillon said.

When he was finished, Harry said, "These Russians, what bastards."

"Never mind that," Billy interrupted. "What's the real word on Hannah?"

"Bellamy says he's sure she'll make it, but she'll never be the same again."

"And Ferguson?" Harry demanded.

"I told you. He took a slug from an AK. He won't die from it, but at his age . . ." Dillon shrugged.

"And Selim out of it." Billy shook his head. "That's a waste. He could have said a lot."

"He came round in the end. Coughed up plenty."

There was a silence. Harry turned to Dora. "A little Bushmills, here, love. I think we're going to need it." He turned back to Dillon. "So Belov's at this Drumore Place, and Ashimov and the girl have joined them, plus the two IRA gangsters?"

"That's it."

"And you can't touch them because they're in the Irish Republic."

"Yes, Harry."

"And they've got a plane to Moscow booked out in the morning? I'd say you're fucked, Dillon."

And Billy, his face as always colder than ice, said, "No, he isn't. You're going in, aren't you? Who else will be there?"

"Discount Regan and Fahy. I'd say there's Kelly and Tod. Probably Danny McGuire and Patrick O'Neill. There could be a few more. Then again, times have changed. They could even have cleared off for a while. Kelly has a boat, the *Kathleen,* which looks like rubbish but is hot stuff. He might think a cruise was indicated."

"But the Russians for sure?"

"Belov, Ashimov and the woman. That's all I know for certain."

Billy said, "So you're going on by air?"

"A beach landing, Billy."

"You're mad, Dillon," Harry said.

"Harry, I just don't like what they've done. Ashimov's a butcher, and Belov thinks he rules the world. What they've done to Ferguson and Hannah and that poor silly sod Selim has to be paid for."

There was silence, and Dora brought the drinks. Dillon took his straight down. "Harry, I'm tired. I've been at war with the world for years and it's a darker world than when I started. I'll be honest, though. I came for help from the boy wonder here and I was wrong. He's done enough. In Hazar last year, he got a bullet in the neck, eighteen stitches in his face and his pelvis fractured. I was stupid to think he should be jumping out of a Citation at six hundred feet over Drumore Bay. As for me, though, I don't have a choice. I can't face those bastards walking away from this. It's not an option." Dillon got up.

Billy said, "How many times have we done something like this, Sean?"

"I don't know. It blurs. Three?"

"Well, then, this will make it four." He got up. "Let's get moving."

"Billy," his uncle said.

"Oh, shut up. Let's go, Sean."

In the Great Hall at Drumore Place, Ashimov, Greta and Belov sat beside the log fire burning brightly on the hearth. Belov said, "So Selim is out of the equation, although I wonder just how much he said to Ferguson before he met his end."

"That concerns me, too."

"Having said that, except for the wounding of Ferguson, the rest of the enterprise was a failure. When I put it together with what happened in Iraq, it's hardly been a success, Yuri. And Fahy and Regan! This Dillon has been a thorn in our side since the start. We underestimated him badly." He turned to Greta. "Wouldn't you agree, Major?"

She glanced at Ashimov, but couldn't avoid Belov's penetrating stare. "I went into his past thoroughly. There was no doubt he had a remarkable record."

"And you made your opinion known?"

Again, she glanced at Ashimov. "Yes, I did, particularly to Kelly and his people." As if trying to make up for the damage she was causing, she added, "Kelly and Murphy should have been well aware of what they were taking on. They were close associates of Dillon once. It's not like they didn't see him firsthand."

At that moment, Hamilton, an old man from the village who acted as a kind of butler, came in.

"Excuse me, sir, Dermot Kelly and Tod Murphy are here."

"Are they, now? Show them in."

They sat there waiting, and the two of them entered.

"Back from the wars, I see," Belov said.

Kelly, roused by drink, was aggressive. "We did a grand job for you. We killed Selim and clipped Ferguson."

"And left one of your own men dead and the other

one giving every scrap of information Ferguson wanted in complete detail. Not your best day's work, Kelly."

Kelly was speechless with fury. It was Tod who said smoothly, "These things happen. The fact is we did get Selim, as Dermot says, and we wounded Ferguson. We did our job. Do you need anything else?"

"Yes, we're leaving in the morning for Moscow. I want you and what's left of your men to stand on watch tonight. As to your future—we'll discuss it another time."

Kelly started. "Now, look here."

Tod caught his arm. "That's grand, sir, thank you for being so understanding."

He took Kelly with him out to the hall. "Shut up, Dermot. Our day will come, isn't that what we said in the Provos in the old days?"

"I could kill the bastard."

"Not now. We go down to the Royal George, have a drink with McGuire and O'Neill and then we'll come back and do what Belov wants. It's to our advantage, Dermot, and that's all that matters."

In the hall, Belov said, "So, Moscow tomorrow."

"And then what?" Ashimov asked.

"We see if there are any repercussions and we consider our options." He looked hard at them both. "Mine and yours."

A t Farley Field, Lacey was waiting as they drove up. The first thing he said was, "We're using the Learjet, Sean, no RAF rondels. We're flying into a friendly country, remember? Don't want to give the wrong impression."

"Fine. What about weather?"

"We'll be all right. There's intermittent sea fog in the area, but it'll be low tide, so there's plenty of beach."

"Good enough."

"What about the return?" Lacey asked.

"I'm glad you think there'll be one. Since we don't want any trouble with the Republic, you land at Belfast Airport. Park in the usual high-security patch and make arrangements to receive us."

"When?"

"I don't know. It could be a hard one. On the other hand, the border is open these days. Billy and I should have no difficulty in getting to Belfast one way or another."

"I hope that's a given."

"When have I ever let you down?"

"All right, let's get moving."

In the operations room, the Quartermaster, an ex–Guards sergeant major, waited. There were a couple of AK rifles, stocks folded, on the table, two Brownings and a jump bag.

"The extras Major Roper suggested are in the bag, sir. Your equipment is in the next room."

"Good, we'll get on with it."

When he and Billy reappeared, they wore jumpsuits, boots and single parachutes, the Brownings in shoulder holsters, the AK rifles slung across their chests. Dillon carried the jump bag. The others were gathered at the chart table.

"There it is," Lacey said. "Plenty of sand with the tide low."

"I know it well," Dillon told him.

"There might even be more moon than we'd like, but that chance of sea mist could help you. Mr. Salter tells me he's coming along for the ride. Is that all right?"

"No, it isn't," said Billy. "Sorry, Harry. I've got enough on my mind."

Harry looked resigned and hugged him. "You young bastard. You look like you're in a Vietnam War movie."

"You've said that before," Billy told him.

"Go on, get out of it." As Billy went up the steps, Harry nodded to Dillon. "As for you . . ."

"I know. Bring him back, or else."

He followed Billy into the Lear. Parry closed the Airstair door. They settled down, unclipping the parachutes and putting the rifles to one side. The Lear started to roll down the runway.

"So here we go again," Billy said. "Are we supposed to be some kind of heroes or something?"

"No, Billy," Dillon said. "We're handing out rough justice, the kind of thing other people can't face up to. Let's leave it at that."

"Maybe you have a point."

"Oh, I do, Billy." Dillon took half a bottle of Bushmills from a pocket, unscrewed the cap and drank. "To you and me, Billy, the only truly sane men in a world gone mad."

15

At Rosedene, Ferguson woke up to find Roper seated at his bedside in his wheelchair reading the *Evening Standard*. Ferguson took a deep, shuddering breath and Roper, alerted, pulled the alarm button. It was the matron herself who hurried in.

"Now then, General." She raised him, plumped up the pillows and eased him back. "A little water."

She passed the container, he sucked on the straw. "How was it?"

"Some of the best work I've seen Sir Henry do. Twenty-two stitches and the bone was chipped." She had known him many years and used the privilege. "If I may say so, you're a bloody old fool to put yourself in such situations at your age."

"I consider myself reprimanded. What about Superintendent Bernstein?"

"Sir Henry's gone over to the Cromwell. Professor Dawson's in charge now. She couldn't be in better hands."

"Excellent. Will you be serving supper later? It's always so good here."

"Well, we'll see. The best I can manage for the moment is a nice cup of tea." She turned to Roper. "And you, Major?"

"It's better than penicillin, and I'm proof of that."

She went out, and Ferguson said, "Fill me in. He's gone, I suppose?"

"He certainly has, General, and taken young Billy Salter with him."

"Tell me." Roper did, and afterward Ferguson said, "It's a kind of madness that gets into Dillon. He and Billy against at least four IRA old hands, plus Ashimov and the woman—and she can pull a trigger with the best of them—and Belov himself. He's capable of anything."

"I know, sir."

A young nurse brought tea on a tray and poured it. Ferguson went on, "There could be more. It's an old-fashioned IRA area, Major, that sort of place."

Roper sipped his tea. "Don't forget, though, sir— Sean Dillon is a legend to many of those people."

"Yes, I suppose so. Still, I'd feel easier if I could talk to him. Is that possible?"

Roper lifted a kind of handbag. "I have a Codex Four

in here. As you know, you can use it even on an aircraft in flight."

"Then get Dillon for me."

Roper said, "It's me. Where are you?"

"Halfway across the Irish Sea. How's Ferguson?"

Roper told him. "I'm putting him on."

Dillon said, "I'm glad you're in one piece, Charles."

"Oh, never mind me. It was worse on the Hook in Korea when I was eighteen."

"Which would mean you're past your sell-by date, Charles. Time to consider."

"Cheeky bugger. You're hardly a spring chicken yourself, and you're going into harm's way again."

"Can't help it, it's my nature."

"Then think of the boy. Young Salter's been through the mill if anyone has."

"It's his nature, too, Charles. He's a warrior."

"Only the two of you," Ferguson said. "It's not on, Sean."

"Well, it will be in about fifteen minutes. What about Hannah?"

"In good hands. But about her future in our line of work—I don't know."

"Well, there you go. Give me Roper."

Ferguson did. "Sean?"

"Fifteen minutes. Almost a full moon, as it happens, but sea fog below. Lacey will make one pass at six hundred."

Roper felt a shiver go through him. "Take care, Sean."

Dillon laughed. "Nobody lives forever. I'll be in touch. Sounding off."

In the Great Hall, Belov, Greta and Ashimov sat at the huge dining table and worked their way through a roast duck, old Hamilton standing by as the wine waiter.

"Excellent," Belov said. "Mrs. Ryan has just served me a better duck than the Ritz Hotel. Will you tell her that, Hamilton?"

"She's gone, sir, home to the village, leaving strawberries and cream for your afters."

"So you're the only person left in the castle?"

"Well, all the daily staff have gone, sir. They'd rather be out of it. It's a feeling people get. Dermot, Tod and two of their boys are here, finishing off Mrs. Ryan's leftovers in the kitchen."

"Would you like to go home?"

"I think I would, sir. It's like the old days. They're sitting eating and drinking with rifles all over the place."

"Well, off you go, then. Check in at breakfast time and tell Murphy to come and see me." Hamilton scurried out, and Belov said, "Now, why would things be so disturbed? Have you got a theory, Major?"

Greta said, "Not really, sir."

Belov poured a glass of port and lit a Russian cigarette. "It's as if Kelly and company are expecting somebody. Do you think they know something?"

Tod Murphy came in, an AK over one shoulder.

"Good, I'm glad to see you're prepared," Belov said.

"For what, sir?"

"Don't fool with me, Mr. Murphy. It could only be for one man."

At that very moment, they heard the sound of a plane passing very low. They all looked up instinctively. Belov said, "Why, there he is."

Tod turned and ran out, and Ashimov said, "No, it can't be."

It was Greta who said, "You only had to read the files. I kept saying that, but nobody would listen."

On the Lear, Parry had left the cockpit and helped Dillon and Billy to put their parachutes on and rearm themselves. "Seven minutes," he said. "We'll still stick to six hundred. There's heavy ground fog but clear beach below, and the tide is well out."

He turned as Lacey throttled back to almost stalling speed, opened the door and dropped the steps. There was a huge rush of wind.

Dillon moved forward and turned to Billy. "We should do this more often."

Billy said, "Get the hell out of it," pushed and dived after him.

They descended, the moon above, into the fog at six hundred, then swung clear at two hundred and there was the sea, the beach, the harbor in swirling fog, a handful of boats and Kelly's *Kathleen* tied to the end of the jetty in the channel.

Dillon made a perfect landing, punched his quick release, didn't even have to roll, glanced over and saw the other parachute billowing, just clear of the tidal surge. Dillon stamped on it, and Billy unclipped and stood up.

"It's coming in," he said. "We'd better get moving."

Dillon said, "Toward the jetty."

"Why?" Billy demanded.

"I want to check that boat of Kelly's," and he led the way, half running, the jump bag in his left hand.

The fog swirled, half obscuring the village, a few lights gleaming through from the Royal George. The *Kathleen* was tied up at the end of the jetty. Dillon said to Billy, "Just keep an eye out. I'll only be a minute."

"What are you up to?"

"Never mind."

Dillon went over the rail, checked the wheelhouse, then went aft, carrying the jump bag with him. He got what he wanted from it, then took off the engine hatch and did what he had to do inside. He replaced the hatch.

"Come on, Dillon," Billy hissed. "What in hell are you doing?"

"Just immobilizing the engine," Dillon said. "Now let's get moving."

They started up through the village.

On the terrace, Kelly and Tod, Ashimov and Belov stood in the darkness, Greta behind them. Belov searched the bay through night glasses and caught the two pale mushrooms descending out of the fog.

"Parachutes—two."

He passed the glasses to Ashimov, who looked for a few moments, then caught a clear glimpse of Dillon's face when he and Billy moved to the end of the jetty.

"Dillon." He passed the glasses to Tod.

"We'll take the bastard now," Kelly said.

"No." It was Belov who spoke. "An old rule, Mr. Kelly. Let the enemy come to you."

Which was fine except for the fact that Dillon had produced a pair of night glasses himself and caught them on the terrace.

"They're there, Billy—Tod, Kelly, Belov, Ashimov and the girl—and they've seen us."

"You think that's the lot?"

"No, at the least there would be McGuire and O'Neill, maybe more."

"Is that all?" Billy laughed. "Let's get on with it."

They moved out from the jetty, turned into a narrow cobbled street and started up the slope toward the castle.

In the hall, Tod Murphy took charge. "We'll draw them in by leaving the French windows of the library at the east end of the grand terrace open, also the windows at the western end, that's the drawing-room end, open. You take the library, Danny," he said to McGuire. "There's a trellised summerhouse there. You wait and try to get them from the back as they pass, making for the windows. You, Patrick," he said to O'Neill, "do the same thing at the other end by the dining room."

"And what about us?" Ashimov demanded.

"You wait in the library and you in the dining room, Dermot," he said to Kelly. "Catch them in cross fire."

"And me and Major Novikova?" Belov asked.

"I'll stand back with you as guard at the rear of the Great Hall until it's all over."

"Well, let's get on with it," Kelly said. "Sort the bastards out once and for all," and they dispersed.

Billy and Dillon crouched together, fog swirling, a slight drizzle falling. Dillon looked at the terrace through his night glasses. "Not very bright. They've left the windows open to draw us in. Have a look. There's a movement in that trellised summerhouse, and look at the one to the right."

"Very naïve," Billy said. "What do you want to do?"

"I think there's someone waiting inside the house as well. We'll do it our way," and he quickly explained.

McGuire, waiting nervously in the little summerhouse, peering out, didn't hear a thing, and was aware only of an AK nudging him in the back.

Billy said, "Make a sound and I'll blow your spine apart. Now, be good and tell me who's in the library and who's wherever else."

"The Russian, Ashimov," McGuire said. "Kelly's in the dining room and Tod's in the Great Hall with Belov and the woman."

"Good man," and Billy rammed the stock of his AK into the base of McGuire's skull.

A moment later, Dillon rejoined him. "I got O'Neill. It seems Kelly's in the dining room. I'll try and trace him."

"Are you sure?"

"We'll see."

They moved cautiously toward the other end of the terrace. Dillon crouched at the balustrade and called softly, "Are you there, Dermot? It's me, Patrick. We've got a problem."

He intensified the distinctive Northern Irish accent even more, and it produced a result. "What is it, you stupid eejit?" Kelly whispered back and moved into the open windows, where Dillon immediately shot him, the silenced AK making only a muted cough. Billy moved in close.

"Now what?"

"Leave Ashimov and go in through the dining room. I know this place. They keep the cars at the front of the house in the courtyard. I'll go round, make sure they can't be used, then enter by the front door. I'll kick up the kind of fuss that will flush Ashimov out, and you can get him from the rear."

"I'm your man."

Billy stepped over Kelly's dead body and Dillon faded into the darkness.

Tod, in the shadowed archway at the end of the Great Hall, stood between Greta and Belov, a Browning in his hand with a twenty-round magazine protruding from the butt.

"It's too quiet," Greta said.

"It always is," Belov told her.

"I knew this was bad news from the start," Tod said. "I think we should get out now, grab one of the cars and go for Ballykelly."

"A man after my own heart," Belov said.

Greta panicked and called out, "Yuri, where are you?"

"Don't be stupid," Tod told her and opened the front door.

Dillon, who was removing the ignition key from the last of the four cars, swung and put a short burst into the brickwork at the side of the door.

"Is it yourself, Tod? No way out here."

"Damn you, Dillon," Belov called, and Tod kicked the door closed.

"Follow me," he said. "We'll get out through the kitchen tunnel."

"And then what?" Belov demanded.

"The boat, the *Kathleen* down at the jetty. Come on, this way."

"But what about Yuri?" Greta demanded.

"He'll have to look after himself," Belov said. "Now, get moving."

Ashimov, alerted by the noise at the front of the house, moved cautiously into the corridor from the library. At the same moment, Dillon kicked in the front door, went in low, straight through the archway to the Great Hall, and called out.

"Billy?"

Ashimov erupted, firing his pistol, plucking at Dillon's sleeve, a second round catching the stock of his AK, sending it hurtling from his hands. At the same moment, Billy shot Ashimov in the left shoulder, spinning him around, and then shot him again in the heart.

"Are you okay?" he called to Dillon.

"Thanks to you."

"Have Tod and the others cleared off by car?"

"No, I've got all the keys. I've an idea he's banking on another form of transportation. Let's see."

He led the way through the Great Hall to the library and the terrace beyond. There were only wisps of fog now and the moon was incredibly bright, the village below, the houses, the inn, like cardboard cutouts. Tod, Belov and Greta had emerged from the walled garden and were hurrying down the lane.

"What's going on?" Billy demanded.

"They're making for the *Kathleen*. It's always ready for sea, that's been the way of it with Kelly for years."

"But they're getting away," Billy said, as he saw them scramble over the rail of the boat. Belov and Greta cast off and Tod went into the wheelhouse. The engine coughed into life, and the *Kathleen* started down the channel.

"Not really. Haven't you observed, Billy, that you never really get away from anything in this life?"

The *Kathleen* passed the point, and produced a bow

wave as Tod increased speed. Dillon took a Howler from his pocket, pointed and pressed the button. There seemed to be a moment of hesitation, and then the whole vessel split apart in a huge ball of fire. What was left went down like a stone.

"Christ Almighty." Billy turned to him. "Semtex?"

"It was Roper's idea."

"Pity about Greta Novikova."

"She shouldn't have joined, Billy, if she wasn't willing to take the risks. Maybe I shouldn't have joined either, maybe you shouldn't have. I expect our day will come." Dillon smiled wearily. "For the moment, let's get out of here. There are four vehicles in the courtyard and I have all the keys. Two hours to Belfast, and then to home."

Three or four minutes later, they were driving out of the main gate in a Land Rover, leaving Drumore Place, dark and somber, behind them.

EPILOGUE

As the Lear lifted off at Belfast after midnight, Dillon took out his Codex Four and called Roper. There was an instant reply. He said, "Don't you sleep?"

"Not all that much. Where are you?"

"In the Lear. Just lifted off from Belfast."

"Is Billy all right?"

"Saved my bacon. He's just tipped his seat and gone to sleep. What about Ferguson and Hannah?"

"He's been feverish and is now drugged up to his eyeballs. I'm very comfortable in the corner of his room. As I said, sleep doesn't come naturally to me anymore."

"And Hannah?"

"Oh, Dawson did marvelous work, but the truth is she won't be what she was."

"Will any of us?"

"So what happened?"

"We got a superb drop in the fog by the boys, then we checked out the *Kathleen*. You were right about that, so I did as you suggested and we went on to the castle."

"And?"

"We left McGuire and O'Neill in a bad way. I got Kelly permanently. Ashimov almost finished me, but the boy wonder shot him and saved me."

"And the others?"

"They cleared off to the harbor and the *Kathleen*. I let them make it beyond the point, then used the Howler."

"That must have been quite a sight."

"You could say that. I was sorry about Novikova. She saved my life in Iraq."

"Only because it suited her."

"I suppose you're right. We took a Land Rover from the castle, then drove straight up through the border to Belfast. There's nobody there these days. All the old barriers are still there, but no troops, no police, you drive straight through. What in the hell did it all mean?"

"Come home, Sean," Roper told him. "Just come home."

"Very comforting," Dillon said. "Give Ferguson my love."

He sat there, thinking about it all, then opened the bar box, took out half a bottle of Bushmills and poured some into a plastic cup.

Billy, eyes still closed, said, "You're big on moral philosophy, Dillon. Do you believe everything's for the best in the best of all possible worlds?"

"Billy, old son," Sean Dillon said, "believe that and you'll believe anything."